HIGH VERMILION—
THE TOUGHEST TOWN IN THE WEST

The saloon was a boiling riot, pick handles slashing down in the murky dimness.

A pair of miners were slugging it out with the bartender on the bar top. Tables and chairs were smashed, the piano dumped on its face. Every man in the room dived into the brawl.

Moffat looked at the brutal carnage and grinned. It wasn't his fight. At least that was what he thought.

Then his hidden past turned up—and a hundred greedy men with guns started to come down on him . . .

HIGH VERMILION

Luke Short

BANTAM BOOKS
TORONTO • NEW YORK • LONDON • SYDNEY • AUCKLAND

HIGH VERMILION

*A Bantam Book / published by arrangement with
Houghton Mifflin Company*

PRINTING HISTORY

Serialized in SATURDAY EVENING POST *May-July 1947*
Houghton Mifflin edition published March 1948
Bantam edition / July 1949
New Bantam edition / 1956

2nd printing ..... April 1956	6th printing .. December 1972
3rd printing ... October 1960	7th printing ...... May 1973
4th printing .. September 1967	8th printing .. November 1979
5th printing .... August 1972	9th printing ... February 1987

ISBN 0-553-26423-0

Published simultaneously in the United States and Canada

*Bantam Books are published by Bantam Books, Inc. Its trade-
mark, consisting of the words "Bantam Books" and the por-
trayal of a rooster, is Registered in U.S. Patent and Trademark
Office and in other countries. Marca Registrada. Bantam
Books, Inc., 666 Fifth Avenue, New York, New York 10103.*

PRINTED IN THE UNITED STATES OF AMERICA

KR   18 17 16 15 14 13 12 11 10 9

HIGH VERMILION

1

BEHIND HIM, the lingering heat from the assay furnace touched his back with a welcome warmth for this high-country September night. Larkin Moffat ceased his writing now. He lifted both big hands from the rough deal table on which he'd been working and, his black brows drawn straight in a frown of concentration, reached past the kerosene lamp and released the catch on the delicate glass-cased set of sample balances beyond.

Now that he was no longer touching the table, the sensitive balance needle moved swiftly, accepting its burden, and slowly settled into immobility. Moffat read the gauge, removed the sample, locked the balance, made his calculations rapidly, signed his name on the report, and then rose immediately, as if an unwelcome chore were done.

He stretched tremendously, so that his tall, lean frame rose toward the low rafters of this small log room. He felt the movement peel his sweat-dried wool shirt from the skin of his back. At the same moment he heard the team and buggy turn off Vermilion's main street and begin the ascent of the boulder-strewn mire of a road that passed his shack and vanished in the timber above. His watchful, taciturn face was touched momentarily with a livening interest as he thought, *How does a man take news like this?*

Reaching for the curved-stem, charred pipe among the papers on his desk, he put it in his mouth and turned back into the cluttered room, hearing the team halt outside. He moved past the assay furnace, to his plank bench scattered with the molds, sample sacks, flux bins, tongs, and cupels that he had not had time to clear away, and was hunting some matches when the man spoke from the doorway.

"Finished, Moffat?"

The voice held an undertone of excitement, and Moffat turned to regard Dutch Surrency. He was a blocky man in a dark clay-stained suit and muddy boots, and his gray-shot, roan spade beard hid most of his face except the button nose and the dark eyes as full of suppressed excitement as his voice had been.

Moffat inclined his head and said, "There it is on the corner of the table, Dutch."

Dutch Surrency moved into the room almost reluctantly, and reached for the assay report. There was a moment of absolute stillness while he examined it, and then Dutch Surrency breathed softly, "Well, the Lord love Jesus!" His glance, wild with amazement, lifted swiftly to Moffat, and then he wheeled toward the door, this time in a hurry.

"Candace!" he bawled out into the night.

Moffat heard the sound of a weight hitting the cinders at his doorstep, a rustle of dress goods, and then Candace Surrency came swiftly through the door. She gave Moffat the briefest of smiles and then took the report her father was extending to her and glanced at it.

Watching her, Moffat saw the same stunned amazement come into her face, which was already flushed with expectancy. A shining, almost childlike delight was in her deep brown eyes as she raised her glance to her father. Impulsively now, she hugged him, and the wool shawl she had thrown over her shoulders dropped to the floor. Moffat put a match to his pipe now, feeling an envy he thought was long dead stirring faintly within him.

Candace broke away from her father and Moffat saw the tears of happiness in her eyes. She, a pretty girl in her middle twenties, not tall, with none of the plain and rugged boniness that seemed the mark of survival in most of the women of this mountain silver camp. Her pale hair, fine and curling and brushed away from her face, was threaded with darker hair the color of her straight eyebrows, and she wore a simple gray housedress with an unconscious regality that made Moffat think, *She'll wear silks the same way.*

Confusion was in her expression now, and Moffat knew, from experience in these things, that she wanted to thank him, like a king of old rewarding the bearer of

2

good tidings. A spare smile tilted the corner of his wide mouth; he said, "You have a lucky father, Miss Surrency."

"But two thousand ounces of silver to the ton?" Candace asked slowly. "You couldn't be mistaken?"

Her father cut in promptly, gruffly, "Hell, girl, never ask an assayer that. He'll shoot you dead." His beard moved in a smile and now he said abruptly, "Look. We've got the whole world to move. Take the buggy and find a kid and send him into the Silverbell for Spence. Take Spence down to the shack. I'll be along in a minute."

Candace, Moffat saw, was blushing now. She glanced almost shyly at him and said, "Hurry, Dad," and said good night over her shoulder as she moved out the doorway.

Moffat listened to her saw the team around, and when the buggy was headed downslope, he shifted his attention to Dutch. Surrency was studying the assay report. Now he laid it down carefully on the table. Pushing his black hat to the back of his head, he put both hands on hips, still staring at the report, and afterward his gaze lifted slowly and settled on Moffat.

"You're going to talk with me, my friend," Dutch said gently. "You know what about, too."

"I can guess."

"You're getting a sixth share in this."

Moffat shook his head. "No. Just my fee."

"Who told me the stuff lay at the crossed fault?"

Moffat said nothing; he smoked passively, only a faint and negligible interest in his sober face. Dutch hauled the chair away from the table, straddled it, folded his arms, and looked searchingly at the room and finally at Moffat.

Dutch said gently, "You can fool some of this camp, Moffat. Why you want to is your own business. Only quit trying to fool me. You're a mining engineer—and a damned smart one."

Moffat took his pipe from his mouth, and said in a quiet voice that was cold in its contradiction, "I'm an assayer."

"Among other things, yes. But you're a mining engineer first. No jack-leg prospector or miner—or assayer—

3

could tell me where the stuff lay. A lot of them tried."

Moffat said nothing. A fleeting irritation crossed Dutch's face and was gone. He said, "Do you know what I'm bucking now?"

"You told me. You've got to get a lot of ore out, and in a hurry."

"That's, so" Dutch said grimly. "I took a six months' lease on the Big Jay in April. I agreed with Jarboe to pay him a seven per cent royalty on every ton of ore I took out. I've worked like a dog and barely made expenses on that low-grade stuff." He paused, and added sourly, "Well, I've struck it rich, and I have just twelve days to work the mine. After that, it reverts to R. B. Jarboe."

Moffat said nothing, and Dutch said sharply, "You listening?"

"I am," and now Moffat's voice held a faint edge as he said, "If every hour counts, why are you wasting one on me?"

"For one thing, it's partly your money."

"I told you, I don't want it," Moffat said wearily.

"Then why in hell did you tell me where to look for it?" Dutch protested hotly. "You've made me a fortune. I was just another customer of yours. Why'd you do it?"

Moffat shrugged and said lazily, "I talk too much."

Dutch regarded him in bafflement for a long moment, and then he raked his chin through his beard with blunt, work-roughened fingers. It made a grating, unpleasant sound in the stillness of the room. He sighed then, and said dully, "All right, then. I'm just too old and too leather-headed to swing it in the time I've got."

Moffat said drily, "You've been mining longer than I have, haven't you, Dutch?"

"That's not the same as fighting," Dutch said.

"Fighting?"

Dutch looked levelly at him. "There's maybe a half-million dollars in silver in that pocket, Moffat. Jarboe owns a couple of mines and the only mill here. A hundred men work for him. When he mills my ore and sees the figures—the money coming out of the mine that will be his again in twelve days—you think he'll let me move that ore? You think he'd rather have seven per cent of it than all of it?"

4

Moffat frowned. "There are ways around that."

"Name one," Dutch said gloomily.

"Keep your assay secret. Don't mill your ore. Lease a patch of ground next to the Big Jay claim and dump your ore on it. All you've got to do is get all the ore you can out of the mine and off Jarboe's property in twelve days. Run four six-hour shifts of the best miners in Vermilion. Pay them anything they ask. Drive them till they drop."

"I am one man," Dutch said dryly. "When do I sleep? Do I watch out for high-grading twenty-four hours a day?"

"Hire a foreman you can trust."

"I'm trying to," Dutch said. "Not a foreman, a partner. Will you boss the job for me for a sixth share and any salary you name?"

"No."

Something close to anger flared in Dutch's eyes, and then vanished. He spoke in a voice he was straining to give a tone of reasonableness, "But why, man, why? You've turned down a sixth share. You've turned down work you can do. What do you want?"

Moffat pushed away from the bench and moved past Surrency to the table. He picked up an opened package of tobacco lying among the papers, and he packed his pipe slowly, with deliberate movements that were almost vicious in their repression. And all the time he was aware that Dutch was watching him closely.

Now he said in a tight, quiet voice, "I don't want the money, Dutch. As for the other, the work, I've been here three months. Nobody cares where an assayer came from or where he's going. But if I took your job, the camp would start backtracking me." He leveled a bleak look at Dutch now. "Once they did that, you wouldn't want me."

Dutch was silent a second and then he murmured, "I see."

"Then if you do, let me alone, will you?" Moffat asked with a hard surliness.

Dutch rose now, a look of hurt and bafflement in his eyes. "Sure," he said, "sure."

He stood there a moment, as if rummaging his mind for words with which to express his feelings, and then,

5

frustrated, he moved toward the door. Checking himself, he picked up the assay report and then glanced obliquely at Moffat. "I'm grateful to you, but I also like to pay my way. You'll get my check for a sixth share, and you can burn it if you want." His voice softened. "Good night, son."

Moffat said good night. He put his pipe down on the desk, and for a moment felt obscurely angry and resentful, and then he moved to the open doorway and put his shoulder against the frame. Through the slot between two buildings where his road left the main one, he looked down in time to see Dutch vanish. A pack train of ore-loaded mules from the Iron Mask mine were wallowing wearily past the slot on the way to the stamp mill, too tired to pick the side of the road where the mud was less deep. His glance lifted beyond them to the creek bottom with its scattering of campfires among the new log buildings and tents, and above them to the close peaks of the Vermilion where a patch of last winter's snow, a cold reminder in the night sky, clung near the highest peaks; and he thought sourly, *I talk too much.*

Immediately, he knew Dutch would never talk, but the conviction remained that he had been a fool to take Dutch's assay. A week ago Dutch was a stranger to him, just another "leaser." In the week since, he had, in a way of speaking, made Dutch rich. And now Dutch had a claim on him, a claim sired by gratitude which would demand of him all those things he did not want to give, things like help, friendship, and interest and enthusiasm. If, on his visit to the Big Jay last week, he had declined the offer of Dutch to look over the workings, this would never have happened. Even if he had looked and said nothing, it still would not have happened. Instead he had talked and argued and discussed, revealing much of the knowledge he had tried to keep secret, and Dutch had shrewdly listened. And now Dutch was rich.

Moffat turned back into the room, unaccountably restless. The appearance of the room fired a deep discontent in him, and he regarded it wryly. It struck him that this shop was a disorderly hole, the board bunk in the airless room behind this one a miserable place to rest. It was as if, in looking at this sorry room, he were looking at his sorry life, and it did not please him. *That's what you wanted, isn't it?* he asked himself.

He remembered then that the stage from Apex was due sometime tonight, and that the shipment of litharge he had ordered might well be on it. This was his excuse to move, and he sought out his coat and his black, straight-brimmed hat, blew the lamp, and stepped out into the chilly night.

At the foot of his road, the street was a bog of churned mud, a deep black now, maroon by daylight, and red when it was dry. He took to it philosophically, and turned upstreet toward the lights of the four corners. Up there, three shots racketed out into the night; there was no commotion following, no shouts, and he paid it little heed, tramping doggedly through the mud.

Like any silver camp barely a year old, the physical shape of Vermilion had not set. It was a formless crazy-quilt of new log stores and cabins, tents, brush huts, and dugouts spread in the shallow valley of Bone Creek. This mire was its main street, strangely quiet, strangely dark for a town that was booming. Moffat knew the reason: the constant drenching rains of summer, the thin, enervating air of this extreme altitude, and the never-distant threat of the coming eternity of winter dogged the camp. Newcomers worked blindly to get shelter against the winter; the barely settled slaved stubbornly to finish assessment work between snows, and the first-comers, with both accomplished, worked only for the wealth that would allow them to leave. Vermilion was a whiskey camp, not a champagne camp.

The main street held a straight line along the slope; on one side a man climbed up steps into the new log buildings, and on the other side he tramped down steps into them. They were spaced irregularly, like broken teeth in a saw.

Ahead of him, Moffat glimpsed the pack train turning up past the hotel on the four corners toward Jarboe's stamp mill on the bald shoulder of Bone Mountain to the east. A cluster of miners, shapeless in their warm clothes and teetering drunk, stood ankle-deep in mud in front of the Silverbell saloon, arguing noisily above the din from the Silverbell's piano. Beyond the four corners, only the lamp of Paxton's livery stable and Beaufort's tent bunkhouse were lighted; the camp, after labor, was mostly asleep and it was far short of midnight.

Moffat angled across the road, dodging a vast pool of wine-colored water, skirted a half-dozen horses at a tie rail, and achieved the top plank of the steps that led down to the Miner's Comfort Saloon on the corner.

A pair of teamsters were staring idly through a dirty window at the ore samples that lined the window ledge of the saloon. They spoke to Moffat as he shoved past them and stepped into the log saloon. The orderly din here, after the silence of outside, seemed, as always, harsh and distasteful.

Moving toward the garish mahogany bar to his right, Moffat wished again that the ceiling of the Comfort were higher. Smoke, the smell of alcohol, the acrid smell of burnt giant powder, the ever-present odor of wet wool and mud seemed to be pressed down and concentrated by the low ceiling.

He moved to the close end of the bar, past its elbow, and put his back to the wall. The bartender, a crippled ex-miner, came up and said, "Stage in yet?"

"Didn't see it," Moffat replied. "Whiskey."

"Hear about Dutch?"

"I heard," Moffat said. The news of a strike could never be kept secret, he knew, but its exact proportions could be. The bartender limped away, and Moffat put an elbow on the bar and regarded the crowd. He liked this exact spot for three reasons; he seldom had to talk with his neighbors, he did not have to stare at himself in the cracked bar mirror, and he could watch the crowd around the angle of the bar. He knew he was developing, at the age of thirty-two, all the crotchets of age, a liking for solitude and a disinterest in his fellow man. Tonight, that suited him.

A half-dozen cowmen, probably on high-country round-up before the fall drive, were drinking quietly toward Moffat's end of the bar. He was watching them when they moved over to let in a man at the bend of the bar, and this man was trailing a half-dozen talkative miners with him. He was slight, wiry with the leaned-down nervousness of a driving man, and his pallid face, deeply grooved at the corners of the mouth, held a cheerful, tough aggressiveness. This was Spence Fuller, Dutch's driller, and he was wearing Surrency's luck like a badge, Moffat saw.

From his stained corduroy coat, Spence took out a battered notebook and slapped it on the bar, and the bartender, bringing Moffat's drink, paused in front of Fuller.

"Dutch hit it, hunh?" he asked, with a grin.

"Right where it feels good," Spence Fuller agreed. He had a startlingly deep voice with a crisp edge of command in it. Now the men from the gambling tables across the room started to drift toward the bar, crowding around Spence. This was the story that never grew old, the story they all wanted to hear, the story that made their gambles reasonable, their grinding work light, and their privations forgotten.

Spence was saying, "Hell, it was at a slipped fault, and Jarboe just plain missed it."

Moffat received his whiskey, and cuddled it in the cup of his hand, listening with a faint apprehension to Fuller's talk. The question he knew would come soon did.

"Who spotted it?" someone asked.

There was a pause, and Fuller said idly, "I don't know. Dutch, I reckon."

Moffat smiled at his drink. That was all right with him; Fuller's evasion had done him a favor.

He felt a man move in beside him and he looked up. The man's broad, high back was to him, face turned to Fuller, but Moffat recognized the shape of Bill Taff. He worked for R. B. Jarboe, with no title or set job, but he was, more than any other man, responsible for the efficient working of Jarboe's half-dozen enterprises. He was chief chore-boy, a lazy-moving, roughly dressed taciturn man, the body for Jarboe's brain.

The bartender saw Taff and greeted him, and spun a glass to him. Taff reached for it and then turned his big head to see who was next to him. When he saw Moffat his broad, bland face altered into amiability; he removed the cigar from his mouth, wiped his full pale mustache with the back of his hand, and said, "How you, Moffat? Some luck, eh?"

"Tough for you and Jarboe," Moffat observed.

Taff shrugged his heavy shoulders. "That's the way it happens. Maybe he'll leave some of it for R. B."

Moffat said nothing and now Taff asked idly, "What did it run to the ton?"

Moffat smiled faintly. "Dutch bought the assay. Ask him."

A fleeting resentment crossed Bill Taff's bleached eyes, but his half-smile remained. "Maybe I better," he conceded.

Spence Fuller's voice overrode the talk now. He was calling cheerfully, "Same deal as I made at the Silverbell, gents. I'm Dutch's foreman now, and I'm hiring any miner who wants five dollars for a six-hour shift; step up and let me look him over."

There was a general murmur of surprise at this announcement; a six-hour shift was unheard of, a five-dollar wage fantastic.

Someone called from the crowd, "You say six hours, Spence?"

"Six hours. The way I'll work you, you'll wish it was four."

There was some laughter then, and the working miners began to push forward toward Spence at the bar. Moffat, watching him, thought Dutch had made a passable choice of a foreman. A cluster of miners who had drifted in from the street to hear Spence and were standing hesitantly around the door now shuffled forward, and Moffat, watching them idly, heard Spence say to the first-comer, "Let me see your hands. All right. Name?"

A tall, rawboned miner had put his shoulder against the door, and Moffat saw him looking over the crowd carefully. His glance slowly traveled the bar and then halted at sight of Taff. Moffat saw him look at Taff a moment and raise his eyebrows in questioning. Moffat was not even sure Taff was watching the man, but now the miner pushed away from the frame, and lurched unsteadily up to the miners waiting for Spence's questioning.

The man was drunk, Moffat judged, and he turned to his own drink and downed it. Liquor, however, could not soothe his restlessness tonight; he laid a coin on the bar and pushed away from the wall, heading for the door and the night outside.

Above the babble of voices, he heard Spence Fuller's

crisp voice say, "No souses on this job, brother. Stay sober two days and then see me. Next."

Immediately, there was the sound of a heavy fist thudding flesh, and Moffat hauled up and looked over his shoulder. The drunken miner had hit Fuller, knocking him into the bar with such violence that the two men next to him had been brought to their knees.

Spence lay sprawled against the bar rail, and now he was struggling desperately to regain his feet for the inevitable fight. The miner, anticipating this, jumped for him, knees drawn high. He landed on Spence's chest then with both heavily booted feet, his knees stiff. Spence's body half lay across the bar rail, and every man in the room heard the anguished shriek of pain from the smaller man.

The tilt of Spence's body had thrown the miner off balance. He staggered and fell on one knee into the crowd. A miner cursed him, and moved away, and now Moffat, sizing this up swiftly, knew Fuller was hurt and would be hurt more.

Without thinking then, he shouldered past a pair of onlookers, and saw the big miner rising to a crouch. Moffat acted swiftly, inadequately, for the miner was moving in again. He kicked out at the miner's nearest leg, catching his ankle with the hook of his booted foot. There was enough weight behind the kick to skid the miner's leg on the muddy floor—spreading his legs widely and shoving him off balance. He fell on his knees, and Moffat moved in on him. He waited until the miner turned his head to see his attacker, and then he lifted his knee into the miner's face with a drive of his leg that carried the miner over backwards and sprawled him on his back.

Moffat said sharply then, "Get out of here before somebody hurts you."

The miner's pale eyes held a cool and calculated viciousness as he scrambled to his feet. *He's not drunk,* Moffat thought. The miner did not even look at Fuller, who was moaning softly against the bar rail; he kept his steady-bright glance on Moffat, and Moffat saw him put his hand inside his jacket. He brought out a long, thin

11

case knife, and without a word began to move in on Moffat.

Moffat backed away, cursing himself for coming away without his gun. The miner was between him and Spence's gun, too. And Moffat knew, without questioning it, that no man here would help him; he had needlessly bought into this fight, and it was his.

Moffat heard men giving way behind him. Backing, he bumped into one of the gambling tables, and he saw the miner, a Finn, he judged, prepare for his rush. Moffat fumbled behind him and touched the back of a chair, and as the Finn laughed, Moffat took a deep step backward and skidded the heavy barrel chair around in a tight circle.

It crashed into the miner's legs and tripped him, and Moffat, waiting for him to go down, came up on his toes. The Finn fell to his knees, but his knife hand was up in front of him, and now Moffat settled back on his heels and backed away past the table. The Finn came to his feet, moving against his legs, and fear touched him fleetingly for the first time; he did not relish closing with the man, and he would have to.

A voice said, "Somebody shoot him," in the quiet of the room. The Finn moved toward him, and Moffat reached out for a near-by chair and pulled it to him, putting it between them.

And then Moffat remembered the ore samples on the window ledge that the teamsters had been idly regarding when he came in. Fumbling behind him, he touched one and lifted it. It was a chunk of spar the size of a shoe, roughly the same shape, and it would do. He lifted the chair, using it as a shield for his body, and lunged at the miner, ramming the chair at his midriff. He knew the Finn would try to brush it aside, and he put the whole weight of his body into the push, keeping the pressure on. The Finn batted the chair with his big hand to clear it from his body, but the chair had come too swiftly. He had it almost clear of him, when a leg punched into the pocket of his jacket, turning him.

Too late now, he gave way, wheeling with the chair, and Moffat let go the chair and moved in, sidestepping, swinging the chunk of spar at the Finn's head with a clouting, stiff-armed motion. His body turned away from

12

Moffat, the Finn's knife was useless. He raised a shoulder to ward off the rock and then it caught him alongside the head.

There was a muffled, subdued report, then, and the Finn was driven forward on his face across the table; he rolled off it onto the floor, and lay slackly where he fell, not moving. The knife was still in his hand.

Breathing deeply, Moffat raised his glance to the silent crowd of men, and, remembering, shuttled his gaze to the end of the bar. Bill Taff was gone.

He said surlily, "Well, somebody help him," and he pushed past the Finn on his way to the bar.

Spence Fuller was conscious; he was breathing lightly, his face drawn with pain. As Moffat approached, a pair of men tried to lift Fuller to a sitting position, but he groaned and motioned them away.

Moffat knelt by him, and saw the sweat beading his forehead, even his eyelids, which were closed.

"Where does he live?" Moffat asked, and looked at the circle of men around him.

Nobody knew, and Moffat frowned in bafflement. Then he said, "Will somebody show me the way to Dutch Surrency's place?"

A miner said he would, and Moffat bent over and picked up Fuller in his arms and rose. The hurt man did not protest; he had lost consciousness.

The crowd parted for Moffat's guide, and Moffat followed him. A curious pair of miners were toeing the Finn over on his back as Moffat passed.

Outside, the miner cut around the Comfort downslope toward the flats of Bone Creek. There were a couple of dark log shacks behind the saloon, then the road fell away into darkness and they took a muddy path through an alder thicket, passing a lighted tent, and presently the guide said, "It's the next place on."

"Go ahead and tell Dutch to get ready," Moffat said.

The miner went on a trot, and, afterward, when Moffat came abreast the shack, Dutch was standing in the doorway.

The guide vanished in the night, and Dutch turned and led the way into his house. Stepping carefully through the door, Moffat saw he was in a large cheerful room that was the kitchen and living room. Candace

Surrency came through a door in the far wall, and motioned silently for Moffat to enter the bedroom.

The lower shelf of a double-decker bunk in a far corner of the small room was made up, and Moffat eased his burden on the clean blankets and straightened up.

Candace, from beside him, asked quietly, "What have they done to him, Mr. Moffat?"

"Broken his ribs, I'd judge."

"I bind him up tightly, then, don't I?" she asked.

Moffat nodded, looking at her. Her glance, grave and untroubled and somehow curious, held his for a moment, and then she moved out of the room. Moffat's glance shuttled to Dutch, who was looking at Fuller from beside the door. Dutch glanced at him and said, "A fight. Who with, though?"

Moffat had no time to answer, for Candace returned with the bandages.

When they had stripped Fuller to the waist and bound his bruised chest tightly in muslin rags, Candace went again to the kitchen, and this time Moffat followed her, knowing that it was time to tell his story. Should he tell Dutch of Bill Taff? But he wasn't sure Taff had played a part in this. He pondered this a moment, until Dutch, who was sitting on the edge of the clean kitchen table, said, "Now, what happened?"

Moffat thought coldly, *This is no affair of mine,* and, only now remembering he still wore his hat, he took it off, saying, "Some drunken miner, Dutch. Spence was hiring, and when he told the man to sober up, the trouble started. He knocked Spence down and stomped him."

Dutch swore. Candace, pouring hot water into a basin at the stove, glanced up at Moffat; he saw a faint, tolerant smile begin on her face, and then vanish.

Dutch rubbed a hard palm over his face and across the back of his neck, and swung down from the table. "Hell of a thing," he growled. "Hell of a time to have it happen." Then he added, "That's what I meant."

Candace said reprovingly, "Spence didn't plan it, Dad," and turned away from the stove with the basin, passing in front of Moffat. Dutch regarded her unsmilingly, his eyes morose, abstracted, bitter, and then he glanced with silent accusation at Moffat.

Moffat shifted his feet, waiting for the few further questions before he could decently take his leave. He looked idly about the room, noting for the first time how clean and scoured this room seemed in contrast to the littered, muddy shelters he was used to in this camp of men. A single colorful plate leaning against the wall on a homely shelf was as pleasant a sight as flowers, but only a woman would think of it, he reflected.

Dutch's next question roused him.

"Who stopped the fight?"

A wariness came to Moffat then, and he thought swiftly, *He'll be thanking me again;* he said, "Nobody. Spence couldn't make a fight of it."

He hefted his hat and said, "I'll be going, Dutch."

Candace's voice, grave and quiet, came from behind him. "Afraid to ask him, Dad? I will."

Moffat half turned, and Candace came up to him. Her dark eyes held a faint embarrassment, a distaste for what was coming. "Dad wonders what I'm wondering. This accident to Spence. It wouldn't make you change your mind?"

Moffat felt his face setting mulishly, and it exasperated him, and he said, "No, not any."

"Is it money? We'll have lots."

"No. It's just out of my line."

Candace hesitated a moment. "Dad says not."

Moffat's glance lifted over the crest of her pale hair to Dutch beyond, and it was bitter and reproving.

Dutch said stoutly, "I said last week I thought you'd had the experience I can use. I still say so."

"I'm an assayer," Moffat said coldly, finally.

A mocking smile, almost challenging, came to Candace's face. She said, "They're quiet, studious men, aren't they? They smell of chemicals and arithmetic books. Do they study about taking knives away from drunken miners?"

An anger stirred within Moffat, and Candace saw it.

She said slyly, "Your miner friend gave you away, didn't he?"

"It looks that way."

"It also looks as if you'd helped us again, whether or not you wanted to. Thank you."

15

Moffat looked down at his hat, a wicked anger in him, and when he said nothing, Candace moved away.

He said, "Well, I'll be going."

Dutch moved away from the table and silently showed him to the door. Opening it, Dutch said with the irrelevance of deep discomfort, "Spence'll be all right, if it's only his ribs."

"Sure," Moffat said. "Good night." He remembered Candace then, and he turned. She was standing by the stove, watching him, a stirring of mischief in her face.

"Good night, Miss Surrency."

"Good night, Assayer," Candace said pleasantly.

Moffat stepped out into the night, and the door closed behind him. He moved away from the shack, swearing softly. He should have walked away from Spence Fuller there at the Comfort; he should never have come here, so this girl could bait him. It was almost as if she knew that he had never wanted to help them, that he was afraid of their friendship.

He plowed abruptly into an alder thicket. Backing out, he took his bearings in the chill blackness. When he started out again, he was still thinking of Candace Surrency, and, oddly enough, more temperately.

Surrency's position, he knew, was hardly enviable. Good drillers, let alone good foremen who would drive good miners, were hard to come by. There was timbering and tramming and mining to be done, the endless breakdowns and emergencies to combat, and unless Surrency could do it himself, he was in trouble. And then Moffat thought, *Why do I care?* and put it from his mind.

The climb in the mud to the street level before the Comfort winded him, and he paused here, breathing hard of the thin cold air. The stage was not in yet; he could see the scattering of curious people still loafing on the steps of the lamplit, two-story log hotel on the opposite corner.

He stood there a moment, irresolute, not wanting to return to the shack, not wanting to wait. And then the question that had been floating in the back of his mind since the saloon brawl, returned to nag at him; had Bill Taff had a hand in the attack on Spence? Was Dutch right in thinking the attack on Spence was planned? Certainly Jarboe, Taff's boss, stood to profit by every delay

16

in moving ore from the Big Jay, and just as certainly, the attack on Spence would delay it. There was a way to find out, he knew, and then it occurred to him that the only person this knowledge could help was Dutch, and he was again irresolute.

But the Finn fought me, he thought stubbornly. *I want to know.*

His decision made, he turned upstreet, cutting toward the upper part of town. He passed Holland's Survey Office, and would have walked into a sign upright if it had not been for the faint light from the night lantern in Paxton's livery office across the street. Passing a vacant, can-littered lot, he saw the long high bulk of Beaufort's vast tent bunkhouse looming to the left. It was merely a big floor on piles, with four half-walls of logs. The upper walls and roof were of gray and much-patched canvas. Here, for a dollar a week, a working miner could come off shift to climb into any empty bunk in the four tiers of them, and find the straw-filled mattress still warm from the previous occupant.

A faint touch of light against the front-wall canvas was the only nightlight in the bunkhouse. There was no door, Moffat saw, but over the door frame he could make out the crudely painted sign proclaiming:

Beds $1.00 a week
No Bugs at This Altitude

He stepped through the doorway and saw, to his right, the night watchman backtilted against the wall in his chair, a lantern on the floor beside him, a sawed-off-shotgun leaned against the wall beside the lantern. He was an old man, and he regarded Moffat with a bland boredom in his eyes as he chewed quietly on a quill toothpick.

"Did they bring a man in here a while ago? Been in a fight?" Moffat asked.

"Three of 'em," the old man said.

"Big tall man—a Finn, I think?"

The watchman removed the toothpick from his mouth and used it as a pointer. "Bottom deck, third from the back, third aisle. Arnie." He added idly, "Don't think because you're past me, you can shack up for some sleep. I'll be back after you."

Moffat tramped past him, and the watchman said in the same bored voice, "No trouble either."

Once away from the door and into this airless room, there was a smell that had almost the density of a liquid, and Moffat opened his mouth and breathed through it. It was a raw, choking smell of sweating, unwashed bodies and unwashed blankets and clothes. There was a sound, too, a living animal sound compounded of sighs, snores, faint groans, and the deep exhausted breathing of men; and as Moffat worked his way down the dark aisle between the high tiers, the wretched lot of these men came to him. Arnie was one of them, and it was hard to blame him for taking money to hurt a man in order to buy liquor with which to forget this squalid life. But Moffat wanted to know.

After stumbling over a succession of boots and heaps of clothes, he reached the back wall. Counting back, he retraced his steps, and then struck a match which he shielded in cupped hands held against his body. The Finn lay asleep in the bunk, face to the room, a massive and bloody bruise covering temple and cheek.

Moffat blew out the match, hesitant, and then, remembering the brawl and his own narrow escape, he moved. Gently, he reached under the wadded jacket that served the Finn for a pillow. As he anticipated, the knife was there.

Drawing it out gently, he held it in his right hand, and then he reached down and fisted the Finn's underwear in his hand and pulled roughly. At the same time he placed the knife against the Finn's chest with a steady and ominous pressure.

He felt the Finn come awake, and then shrink away from the pressure of the knife. Moffat said, "I'm the man who hit you."

The Finn said nothing, pulling away from the knife.

Moffat said in a low voice, "Want me to leave this in your ribs, friend?"

"No," the Finn muttered.

"Then tell me. What were you paid to beat up Spence Fuller?"

There was a pause; Moffat gently increased the pressure on the knife with one hand, pulling the man toward him with the other.

"Two dollars," the Finn muttered.

"Who paid you?"

Again the pause, again the pressure, and this time Moffat felt the knife break skin. The Finn whined, but Moffat kept the pressure on. And then it came.

"Bill Taff."

Moffat released the man, and he fell back into the bunk. Moffat felt for the bunk upright, and when he located it he drove the knife solidly into it, and then shoved the handle sideways. The blade snapped. Moffat threw the piece remaining down the aisle, and moved after it and passed it on his way out.

Once outside, he halted, breathing deeply to clear his lungs and nose of the bunkhouse's stench. *Well, now you know,* he thought, *Are you going to take it to Dutch?* He smiled with surliness into the night. Let Dutch and his daughter find out for themselves; he'd helped them enough.

Upstreet he heard the stage thrashing through the mud, and before he saw it he heard the driver's whiplash and his drawing curses. He moved toward the four corners, and presently saw the stage materialize out of the darkness and pull up in front of the hotel steps.

Moffat yawned; he was tired, and the restlessness was gone. He would pick up his mercury from the stage driver, and by the time he had lugged it up to his shack, he would be tired enough to sleep.

As he approached the hotel, angling across the intersection, he saw the loafers on the hotel steps indulging in the time-honored custom of looking over the newcomers alighting from the stage.

Moffat crossed in front of the stage's lead team, so close to them that he reached out and scratched the forehead of the off lead horse. He had his foot raised to mount the short stretch of plank walk in front of the hotel when he glanced up at the passengers unloading.

And then he halted.

A tall man in boots and clean corduroy suit was talking to the stage driver. Hand on his arm was a girl, tall too; she was dressed warmly against the chill night in a dark, rich-looking suit, and she stood among the other passengers with a faintly bored expression as the man

19

spoke to the driver, saying, "You didn't win it, my friend, but we all figure you tried. Here's the kitty."

He extended something to the driver.

Moffat did not wait to see what it was. He pulled back behind the horses, and now panic was in him. He turned his back, thinking desperately, *If I run they'll notice me.* He hunched his shoulders, and made himself walk deliberately back to the corner of the Miner's Comfort, keeping the stage between himself and the passengers.

Once in the shelter of the Comfort, he pulled back against the wall. He was shaking, and he felt sweat channeling down his side, and he thought frantically, the panic still holding, *I've got to get out of here.* He stilled his breathing and made himself think. With Josephine and Charlie Storrs in this camp, for no matter how long, he would have to get out. A hundred unwelcome memories that had been buried for three years now came crowding into his mind, and he shivered dismally.

Swiftly, he turned and fled down the hill; once clear of the Comfort, he cut across its back lot, and continued steadily across other back lots until he was a hundred yards beyond the hotel. He labored up to the road, and his mind was functioning swiftly.

He'd gather a few things together, close shop, and drift tonight, before there was any possibility of seeing Storrs or his wife. Charlie and Josephine couldn't have come to see him, probably didn't know he was here. *But they'll find out,* he thought bitterly. And that would finish him here, he knew. He'd come as far as he could, had settled in this high, remote camp at a humble job that brought him enough to live on—and yet it had followed him even here. *It'll follow me everywhere,* he thought with a dismal certainty. But that didn't matter now; the thing that did was getting out of here before Charlie or Josephine saw him and talked.

He climbed his own road swiftly, and when he reached his shack he was breathing so hard that he had difficulty in unlocking his door.

Once inside, he moved to the lamp and lighted it, and then headed directly past his cluttered bench for the door in the rear wall.

Here, in his small bedroom, he lit a candle and looked about him. There wasn't much he'd need. Blankets, his gun—he took this down and strapped it on—a razor, a change of shirts.

He was rolling up these items in his blanket when he heard the sharp knock on the door. For a moment, kneeling on the bunk, he froze into immobility, pure panic again in him. Then he thought, *No, not so soon,* and he took a deep, shuddering breath and rose.

Walking out into the room, he saw Bill Taff standing in the open doorway. Bill said, "We're lucky, Moffat. We caught you still up."

Taff stepped aside into the room, and R. B. Jarboe tramped in behind him. Jarboe was a sagging, dirty man whose ageless slack face was always framed with white beard stubble. One loose jowl was paunched comfortably by a cud of tobacco; a thin line of stained spittle trickled from either corner of his mouth, and from his pendulous underlip, and Moffat, seeing this, knew why the kids of the town followed his buggy yelling, "Hello, one-eleven!" His pale eyes, however, held no suggestion of age or frailty; they were as blunt as shiny brass, and only a little darker in color. He was a big mine owner, mine broker, streetcorner banker, and a trader who would and could turn a profit on any machinery that moved or shack that stood up or man that worked.

He looked over the disorderly room and said, pleasantly enough, "I never understood this damn business of assaying. Does it make you a living, Mr. Moffat?"

Moffat didn't answer for a moment; he was trying to stifle his haste, to put a reason to this visit. He said, then, "Only if I keep busy."

Jarboe wheeled with a suddenness that startled Moffat, and went to the door and spat. He turned and went directly to the single chair and slacked into it. Then he removed his hat and laid it daintily on one knee; his white hair was short, uncombed, and he scratched his head with a slow, circular motion as he regarded Moffat.

"Mr. Moffat," he began gently, "I damn seldom beat around the bush. I prefer to beat it up."

Moffat glanced at Bill Taff, whose hard face held a faint and sleepy smile of expectancy.

"I want that assay of Dutch Surrency's," Jarboe said.

"How do you propose to get it?" Moffat asked drily.

"Buy it."

Moffat shook his head. "I don't reckon."

Jarboe nodded slowly, seriously. "Put yourself in my place," he smiled mildly. "The Big Jay is mine. I leased it to Dutch and he says he struck it rich. Now, what kind of a mine have I got? Rich, or just so-so? I've got to know if I'm being bled white or just a dull gray."

"So you can figure if it's worth it to stop Dutch moving that ore?" Moffat murmured.

"Now whatever gave you that idea?" Jarboe asked.

"Spence Fuller was beat up tonight."

"Too bad," Jarboe murmured.

"And cheap. Just two dollars." Moffat was watching Taff. A bland innocence was in Taff's face, and it never left it. He folded his arms and leaned back against the wall.

Jarboe, when Moffat's glance returned to him, was grinning. He said, "You're a thorough son of a gun, aren't you?"

Moffat said nothing. He wished they would go; the urgency to get out of here had never left him, and this visit would come to nothing.

Jarboe said, "What's your price?"

"The same as Dutch's. Ask him."

"I did. He said the price for telling him how many ounces the new strike is running to the ton would be another six months' lease on the Big Jay."

"There's your answer. Good night."

Jarboe leisurely uncrossed his legs, and then crossed them again. "Does a thousand dollars seem too chinchy, Mr. Moffat?"

"Good night, gentlemen," Moffat repeated.

Jarboe sighed. He looked long at Moffat, and then spat expertly, between Moffat's feet. "I've bought better men for less," he observed.

When Moffat still said nothing, Jarboe rose.

Taff said, "He's got a hungry look, R. B. Double it."

Jarboe looked at Moffat and raised his eyebrows. Moffat only shook his head. "Well," Jarboe said, "there are other ways. Dutch has got to mill it."

He walked to the door and went out, not bothering with a good-bye. Taff, however, remained a moment longer, watching Moffat. Then he shoved away from the wall, and observed quietly, "You got a long nose."

"When it smells something bad, it gets longer," Moffat replied. "Keep yours out of my business."

A murderous light flicked in Taff's eyes and then vanished. He stepped out into the night after Jarboe.

Moffat turned back into the bedroom and finished rolling his blankets. He moved purposefully, as if the interview with Jarboe and Bill Taff were already forgotten.

He picked up his bedroll, lifted his saddle from the corner, and dumped them both outside. Then he returned to his work bench, dragged four sacks of ore from beneath, and lugged them outside. Once more he returned, and this time he took a sheet of paper from the desk and wrote across it, CLOSED. Blowing the lamp, he locked the door and spitted the notice on a nail beside it. Then he stacked the four sample sacks against the door; they were Ben Gower's, and he would take them when he saw the office closed.

Moffat took his bedroll and saddle and cut behind the shack to the shed in the rear. Here, lighting a lantern, he saddled his bay gelding, lashed his bedroll to the saddle, blew the lamp, and swung up into the saddle. And then, in a wave of revulsion he thought of what he was doing, and he thought bitterly, *You damned coward.*

He touched the flank of his horse and moved past the shack and down the road. In the slot between the buildings, he was already kneeing his horse to the left, toward the canyon and away from town, when he reined up abruptly. *Why not?* he thought sourly, *I'll never see them again.*

Instead of turning, he put his horse straight across the road and down the hill, and after an interminable time found the trail he wanted.

There was still a lamp lit in Surrency's place. He rode up to the door and leaned out of the saddle and knocked. This time, he would not be baited, nor would he be trapped by talk. He would leave his message and go.

The door opened slightly, and through the crack Moffat saw Candace peering cautiously out into the night.

"It's me, Moffat," he said. "Dutch around?"

The door opened. Candace held a gray wrapper about her. Her pale hair fell deeply below her shoulders, and the light behind her turned it into still fire.

"He's gone up to the Big Jay, Mr. Moffat," she said.

Moffat scowled. The light from the doorway reached only to his hips, and he knew Candace could not see the urgency in his face. He said, "Tell your father to watch Bill Taff and Jarboe. They paid that miner to beat up Spence. Tell him he was right. They'll fight."

There was a long silence, and then Candace said quietly, "What can he do about that?"

"Keep his head up," Moffat said curtly. "Another thing. Jarboe tried to buy that assay off me tonight for two thousand dollars."

"And that too," Candace murmured.

Moffat shifted impatiently in his saddle. "He can guard his dump. Search his miners so they won't smuggle out ore for an assay. He can keep it from Jarboe for a week."

"You have this all figured out, haven't you, Mr. Moffat?" Candace asked gently.

"Why—yes," Moffat said, momentarily surprised.

"Have you figured out a way a sick man can do it?" Moffat scowled. "Spence, you mean?"

"Dad, I mean. He's still carrying grapeshot in the hole in his side. If that miner tonight had stomped him instead of Spence, he'd be dead now. I chop the wood around here, not Dad. Does that show what I mean?"

Moffat shifted uncomfortably in the saddle. "Well, there are men here who——"

"But not you," Candace said gently, mockingly, "I know."

"I'm leaving," Moffat said curtly.

"Not on our account, I hope," Candace said dryly. "We know how to handle a porcupine."

Moffat lifted the reins and said stiffly, "I'm sorry."

"You are, like hell!" Candace said flatly, and she slammed the door with a violence that shook the shack.

2

IN SPITE OF the thin morning sunshine which streamed in the kitchen window, Candace took her shawl from the nail, put it on the table beside the woven willow market basket, and then went to the doorway of Spence's room.

"Warm enough?" she asked.

"I'm fine," Spence said.

"I'll be back in an hour. Why don't you try and sleep?"

"I'll get enough of that," Spence growled. He raised his head off the pillow to look at her, grinned, and lay back, grunting softly and holding his breath as he moved.

Candace went back to the stove, put a chunk of green pine in it to hold the fire, and moved over to the table. She smoothed the bosom of her green dress and touched her hair absently in the timeless gesture of a woman.

"Candace," Spence called.

Picking up her shawl and basket, she again moved into the doorway.

"Stop in and prod Barber about those timbers. Dutch will need them tomorrow."

Candace smiled slowly. "You can't worry the timbers up there, Spence. Now sleep, will you?"

As she turned to go out, she heard Spence swearing under his breath. Outside, the thin air was cool and bracing, filled with the noisy rush of Bone Creek to the west, and as Candace skirted the shack she looked up at the near slope of Vermilion Peak. Below timberline, there was only a faint stain of the aspens' yellow among the scarlet of the scrub oak. The rain had beaten much of the foilage to the ground; the premonition of winter was there.

She took the crooked trail through the alders, walking briskly, and presently came into the Hostetter's clearing. An eight-year-old with taffy pigtails was playing among the guyropes of the gray tent. She smiled at Candace when she saw her and Candace stopped.

"Sadie, you ask your ma if she can let me have a couple of eggs later on. If she says yes, you better start hunting the brush for them."

"I know where one'll be," the girl answered. She got up and disappeared around the tent, and Candace went on. Now, coming out of the creek bottom, she could hear the racket of the town more plainly. From every side, it seemed, came the sound of axe and hammer blows, and as a background for all the clamor was the muted rhythmic pulsing of Jarboe's stamp mill above town.

The road was drying a little, Candace saw. When she had climbed it to the main street, she paused for breath and looked about her, watching the midmorning traffic of the high ore wagons on their way to the mill. Above the buildings, the pine timber on the slope of Bone Peak was spangled with yellow aspen in a spreading piebald effect that was pleasant to see. A miner came out of the Comfort and passed her, touching his hat in greeting.

Candace looked at the Comfort, and was reminded immediately of Spence—and of Larkin Moffat. A sudden embarrassment touched her; she shook her head in mild vexation and moved on across the main street, climbing the side street past the hotel. She'd lost her temper last night with Moffat, and there was no excuse for it. Only, there was something inhuman about a man who would turn up a fortune for someone else and refuse any part of it; who would half kill a man in a fight that wasn't his own, and then turn surly at thanks; and who was content to waste his talents on a job unworthy of them. In some way beyond her understanding, he was flawed, and even the thought of him somehow made her uneasy.

At the fourth log building up the hill, Caslin's meat market, Candace turned in. Three sides of beef hung on hooks against the back wall. Candace bought a roast, asked for some soup bones and was given them, and afterward came back down the hill to the hotel, where she paused on the short stretch of plank walk to watch a ten-horse hitch to a high-wheeled ore wagon and loaded trailer make the turn to the mill above.

The lead team swung wide, almost to the plank steps of the Comfort, and then, with the jerkline, the teamster turned them and began to lay on the whip. He shouted a hoarse mumbo-jumbo of words, and it was only then that Candace realized the man, in deference to her, was not cursing, and was therefore inarticulate.

She turned hastily and went up the hotel steps and inside, smiling faintly to herself as she heard the teamster lay tongue to his teams.

She closed the door and was commanded immediately by a raw female voice, "Clean your boots!"

Candace smiled and went on into the lobby. It was a big room and held a scattering of barrel chairs, in one of which a man was sleeping, hat over face.

Opposite the door was the desk, a man standing up to it, and now he turned to see who had come in. Behind the desk was Mrs. Barber, a big-bosomed, plain woman with a massive face now frowning in deep concentration over something she was reading. She looked up, and when she saw Candace she smiled.

"Candace Surrency! Well, you can track mud like anyone else."

"I left all mine on your walk," Candace said, and she moved across the room. The big man at the desk half smiled and stood aside, and Candace said, "Is Tim around?"

"Those timbers, eh?" Mrs. Barber said. "Well, he's on his way to the Big Jay now. They'll be there this afternoon. How's Spence?"

Candace told her, and they gossiped a brief moment, and then Candace said good-bye and started across the lobby.

"Miss Surrency?"

Candace halted and turned. The man who had stood aside for her conversation with Mrs. Barber now approached. He was a man of thirty, tall, with a broad, smooth-shaven face, and cold and pleasant dark eyes beneath sandy straight hair. He came forward, carrying his hat, and said, "I overheard your name. I'm Charlie Storrs. You're the daughter, or the sister, of the man who made the new strike?"

"Daughter, Mr. Storrs," Candace said.

The man nodded. "I'm a representative of Corona Metals and Mining Company."

Mrs. Barber said, "He's married, Puss," in her brassy voice.

Charlie Storrs looked at her and grinned, and then returned his glance to Candace. "I've only just heard about the strike. I'd like to hear more." He added by way of explanation, "I'm looking over some mining property here for Corona. I don't recall running into the name of Surrency in the Claim Office files down at Apex."

"It's the Big Jay mine, Mr. Storrs. We only lease it. Mr. R. B. Jarboe owns it."

Storrs nodded pleasantly. "I recall the Big Jay. You have a long lease, I hope."

"A short one."

Storrs clucked sympathetically, but his bold eyes were without anything except a lively curiosity. He said, "Silver and some gold, I suppose. What is the assay?"

Candace smiled and shook her head slightly. "Our own business, Mr. Storrs."

Charlie Storrs raised his eyebrows, and then laughed. "Well, well! How do you keep a secret like that?"

"By milling our ore when the lease is up," Candace said. She started to move away. "Mr. Jarboe is the man you want to see, Mr. Storrs."

Storrs, smiling pleasantly, bowed to her, and watched her go out.

"Quite a girl," he observed, turning back to Mrs. Barber.

"The best," Mrs. Barber replied, stoutly.

"Now," Storrs said in a business-like manner, "about this breakfast. My wife isn't feeling well. It would be a great service if she could have breakfast served in her room."

Mrs. Barber put both tremendous arms on the desk. "She looked all right to me last night."

"She is delicate," Storrs said.

"If she's too delicate to come downstairs, she's too delicate to eat," Mrs. Barber said. "No, I'll lug no breakfast up those stairs."

"Then let me."

"And you won't, either. Breakfast is over by two hours," Mrs. Barber said finally. "Anything else troubling you, Mr. Storrs?"

Storrs laughed then. "Nothing except your stubbornness."

Mrs. Barber nodded solemnly. "It troubles me, too, sometimes. Anything else?"

Charlie Storrs shook his head in bewildered negation and turned away from the desk. Checking himself, he walked back and said, "Who is R. B. Jarboe and where'll I find him?"

"A dirty old turkey buzzard," Mrs. Barber said, placidly. "He's got an office around the corner, across from Caslin's meat market on the hill."

Storrs thanked her. Still carrying his hat, he sought the narrow stairs to the right of the desk and mounted to the second story. At the head of the stairs, he turned back toward the front of the building, paused at the end doorway, knocked, and entered immediately.

This was a small corner room, curtainless, plain as a bone, with one deal chair and a rickety washstand the only furniture, besides the white-painted iron bed. Luggage and clothes, mostly a woman's, were scattered about the room.

Josephine Storrs was in bed, but awake. Her dark hair was braided in a long rope, which trailed off over the edge of her pillow. She yawned luxuriously and folded her arms behind her head so they propped her up until she could regard her husband. She was pretty, and she seemed only mildly out of sorts as she regarded him.

"You better roll over and sleep, Josie," Storrs said. "You're getting no breakfast from that hippopotamus downstairs."

"I probably couldn't eat it if I did," Josephine Storrs said lazily. "What a town. Did you hear that teamster swearing a minute ago?"

"No. Learn anything new?"

"Yes and no," Josephine said. "That is, I'm not sure."

Charlie grinned. "I'm off to work. Want anything?"

"Like plug tobacco, you mean? No, thanks." She yawned. "When do we get out of here, Charlie?"

Storrs eyed her coldly. "As soon as my business is done."

"Hurry it, will you?"

"It was you who wanted to come along," Charlie said. "I'll take my own sweet time."

"Go away," Josephine said sullenly. She turned her back to him and settled down under the covers.

Storrs smiled faintly and stepped out into the corridor. He took time to light a cigar before he tramped downstairs and out onto the street steps, where he paused to have a look at the day.

For some reason, probably the altitude, his cigar tasted wrong; he threw it away, and sought the plank walk, turning up the hill at the corner as Mrs. Barber had directed him.

In front of the meat market, he saw the small office across the road wedged in between a log restaurant and a laundry. There was one window, and beside it the door, over which was a sign reading: R. B. JARBOE, Claims, Mines, Leases Bought and Sold.

Storrs thought with a pleasant anticipation, *Not quite so out-at-the-pants as he'd like to have everybody think*, and took to the churned stiff mud of the road.

The door was open and he stepped inside. A rolltop desk was backed against the far wall, Bill Taff on its counter. Jarboe was seated in an ancient swivel chair, his feet on the counter beside Taff. There was a safe in the near corner, a table cluttered with ore samples and tattered mining journals between it and the desk. There was a calendar on the wall behind Taff, a chair beside the desk. Although this camp was little more than a year old, Storrs remembered, this room and everything in it contrived to seem covered with the dust of decades, and to have acquired an ancient dilapidation.

Storrs said briskly, "Mr. Jarboe?"

"Yeah," R. B. said. He made no move to rise, only regarded Storrs with a cautious, pleasant gaze.

Charlie reached in his pocket, extracted a card and moved over to Jarboe, extending it. "I'm Charlie Storrs."

Jarboe took the card and read it. "Uh-hunh," he said slowly. He inclined his head. "Bill Taff."

"Hoddy," Taff said.

"Hoddy," Storrs said.

"What brings you here?" R. B. drawled. "You Corona fellas shopping around?"

Charlie laughed expansively. "That's the word for it. We like to look 'em over and pick up the missed bets."

R. B. rubbed the white beard stubble on his chin. "Well, you come to the right place," he said dryly.

"So I heard," Charlie replied and he grinned. Jarboe grinned too, but his grin was not as sheepish as it might have been.

Bill Taff reached out and shoved the chair toward Storrs, who accepted it, saying, "That's what I came about. What's Surrency turned up?"

Jarboe looked obliquely at Taff, and then at his scuffed and muddy boots, and then at the knees of his unpressed trousers. He flicked off some dried mud from his left knee, and then looked at Charlie. "I wisht I knew."

Charlie frowned in puzzlement.

Taff said, "Surrency kept his assay secret. You know as much about it as R. B."

Charlie looked in surprise at Jarboe. "Why, you own the mine, don't you? He can't keep you off your own property."

"He can keep me from taking out enough ore for an assay," Jarboe said calmly. "Any ore moved out of there is his, minus my royalty, under the terms of the lease."

Charlie scowled and crossed his legs. "Ever thought of selling the Big Jay, Mr. Jarboe?"

"Up to yesterday I did. Now, I don't know. If he's got a pocket, he'll likely clean it out before his lease is up. If he's turned up a big body, I'll get it. Trouble is, even if I wanted to sell it now, I don't know what it's worth." Jarboe's cheek was beginning to pouch, his voice to thicken. He leaned over and spat into a rusty spittoon on the floor beside him, and when he spoke next, his voice was firm. "I'll sell anything. You Corona people want to buy?"

Storrs, with disarming frankness, then told him the object of his visit. As field man for Corona Metals, he traveled a lot of the time, looking over mine properties. What they were after was a big body of low- to medium-grade ore. If they could find enough of it around Vermilion—for instance, four or five claims working in roughly the same geological formation—and the owners were willing to sell, then a satisfactory price could be arranged and the company would move in the big machinery. Big machinery could make it pay; a lot of little machinery couldn't.

This was sparring, and Storrs knew it and Jarboe knew it, but it was the necessary preliminary, and Jarboe listened gravely. Storrs went on to tell him that he had spent the last two days in the county seat, Apex, twenty miles down canyon, examining records, claims, ownership, assays and verifying the information on the Vermilion camp that Corona had collected previously. For instance, Charlie said placidly, Corona knew all about the Big Jay, the formation they were working, the amount of ore in sight, the value of the equipment, and the quality of ore. The same facts were known about the adjoining mines and claims. Provided Jarboe and his neighbors were willing to put their property up for sale,

Storrs was authorized to check the body of ore, the workings, and open negotiations.

"Trouble is," Charlie finished, and now he was frowning, "if Corona comes into the Vermilion field at all, we want it settled now, this trip. That's what I'm here for. But I won't talk price on a mine I can't look at, and whose ore I can't assay."

Jarboe looked at Taff, and Bill Taff's square sleepy face seemed troubled. Neither spoke.

"Did Surrency run his own assay?" Charlie asked.

Jarboe shook his head. "Fella down the street did it for him."

Taff said, "We tried to buy it from him. He wouldn't sell."

Charlie grunted. "I can look at the Big Jay property, can't I?"

Jarboe nodded, and now Charlie rose. "All right, then, let's go find the assayer. He might change his mind if I promised him all the Corona work for a couple of years. What do you think?"

"I've quit thinking about it," Jarboe said mildly.

"Where is he?"

Bill Taff slid off the desk and walked to the door, and Charlie, saying he'd see Jarboe later, followed Taff.

At the hotel corner, Charlie offered Taff a cigar, which was accepted; they both fired up, and then took to the mud of the road. Charlie noticed that the mud, as it dried, was turning to a red clay. Everything was covered with it—the wheels of the wagons, the legs of the horses, the boots of every man he met. The buildings close enough to the street to be splashed by the wagons were tinted with it. *I'll even bet Josephine picks some of it up on her skirts before she leaves,* he thought sardonically, and then grinned at the thought.

He regarded Taff obliquely, wondering about the man. He must work for Jarboe, but in what capacity Charlie couldn't guess. All in all, this was a curious situation with the Big Jay, and he could sympathize with Jarboe. The man didn't know how much money he was losing each day. That reminded him of something, and he asked, "How long does Surrency's lease run?"

"Eleven more days," Taff said. He gestured now to an alley running between a shoemaker's shop and a bakery.

"We go up here."

Storrs turned into the alley, and again Taff gestured to a shack perched on the rising slope of the hill above the shoemaker's shop. "That's his place."

"What do I call him?" Charlie asked idly.

"Name of Moffat—Larkin Moffat."

Charlie halted in midstride, and stared at Taff. Taff went on a few steps, then halted too, and turned to look at Storrs.

"Did you say Larkin Moffat?" Charlie asked unbelievingly.

Taff took the cigar from his mouth. "That's right. Know him?"

"Tall, black-haired, thick black eyebrows, little scar on the bridge of his nose, light green eyes?"

"That's him."

"Well, I'll be eternally damned!" Charlie Storrs said softly, as if to himself. He smiled, and then began to laugh quietly, a look of honest malice coming into his face. "So this is where he came? Josephine will never believe it."

"You folks know him?"

"We did," Charlie said flatly. "We do. He's a blackleg crook, my friend. I wouldn't pay him to assay a tin cup."

A curiosity stirred in Taff's eyes, and he said, "Crooked how?"

"He worked for Corona, too. That was three years ago. He was one of our top men, and we were buying a lot of property. We got a tip on a prospect at Leadville, and we took a short option, then sent one of our men in to look it over and make tests. He reported it wasn't worth bothering with. We couldn't believe it, so we sent Moffat in. He reported the same, only worse. We took his word for it. The day the option lapsed, Pacific Shares moved in and bought it. Maybe"—and here Storrs's voice turned dry and thrusting—"you've heard what they bought. The Sultana."

Taff whistled in exclamation. "He missed that?"

"On purpose," Storrs said. "Pacific Shares bought him off, and the man before him. Forty thousand dollars apiece. The other man blew his brains out a year ago. Moffat disappeared."

Taff listened in silence, and when Storrs was finished

he smiled meagerly and observed, "Well, well." He looked up at the shack, and then murmured, "Want to meet him?"

"I'd like to," Charlie said, a grim anticipation in his tone.

They tramped up the rocky road in silence. Halting in front of Moffat's door, they saw the sign by the door, and then the sample sacks leaned against the door.

"That's funny," Taff murmured. "He was here last night. We talked with him."

Charlie Storrs frowned, and was silent a moment. Then he asked, "What time?"

"Eleven or so."

"After the stage got in?"

Taff scowled thoughtfully, and then his face cleared. "Right after. I talked with Connie Masters when he was unloading the stage boot."

"I saw you," Charlie Storrs said. A wicked grin came to his face. "Well, Taff, he saw me and my wife and ran. He knew we'd turn him up and he ran." He paused, and added grimly, slowly, "I don't think he'll be back—not if I know Moffat."

Taff glanced at him speculatively, and moved over to the door. He tried it, and then, pulling out his gun, he held it against the lock and fired. Backing off, he raised his foot and kicked savagely at the door. On the second kick, it flew open, and Taff, without a look backwards, entered.

Curious, Charlie Storrs followed him, halting in the doorway. Bill Taff first moved to the desk, saying, "He might have left the assay lying around." Taff began to paw through the papers on Moffat's desk, and Charlie Storrs looked about the disorderly room. His attention returned to Taff, and then shifted to the balances. Lying there inside the glass frame in a sample dish was a small gold button. Charlie glanced at it, and then at the desk, and suddenly he came erect and said, "Hold on a minute, Taff."

Bill looked up.

"Was this Surrency assay the last job Moffat did?"

Taff thought a moment. "Yeah. Dutch got the assay around nine o'clock last night. Sent for his driller in the Silverbell when I was there."

34

Charlie took a step into the room. "You wouldn't know the size of the sample Surrency brought to Moffat?"

"A fifth assay ton," Taff said promptly. "I heard Spence say."

Charlie moved over to the desk and glanced down at the papers. There were figuring sheets, filled with meaningless numbers.

Charlie said softly, "Don't touch a thing."

Ignoring the papers, he unlocked the scales. Then he removed the tiny gold button, and holding it in his hand, weighed the sample dish. Then he placed the button on the dish and weighed it. It took the indicator a time to settle, and Charlie watched it patiently. He said then, "Remember this. Three point seven nine six milligrams."

Now he moved over to the figuring sheets on the table and stared at them. At last he said, "Hah," and looked up at Taff, satisfaction in his face.

"Know anything about assay work?"

"Nothing," Taff said.

Charlie held up the figuring paper. "See that figure. That's the weight of the gold button I just weighed. It checks, doesn't it?"

Taff read it and said, "That's what you read off."

"See the figure above it? That's the weight of the silver and gold button together that Moffat cooked out of the sample. He put that silver and gold button in nitric acid, and the acid dissolved the silver. Nitric doesn't touch the gold. I've weighed the gold. If I subtract that figure from the weight of the button, I know how much silver the acid ate away, don't I?"

He didn't wait for an answer. He picked up a pencil that lay on the desk, and made his subtraction on the figuring paper.

He came slowly erect, then, a look of amazement on his face, and then glanced over at Taff. "Four hundred ounces of silver to the fifth ton," he said slowly. "That's two thousand ounces of silver to the ton." He paused and said solemnly and respectfully, "Your Surrency will be a rich man."

Taff's mouth twisted in a quiet curse, and then he swept the papers from the desk with a bat of his hand. Wordlessly, now, he wheeled and went back into Moffat's room and stood in the doorway a moment, brooding wrathfully. When he turned, his face was stiff with a deep rage.

Beside the workbench stood a buckboard. It was a stout, metal-topped table on which ore samples were crushed. Its muller, a flat-faced sledge with an axe handle, lay atop it, and now Taff, seeing the muller, picked it up and hefted it.

Now he looked at Charlie Storrs, his pale eyes wicked, and then swung the muller down on a cluster of retorts. He moved on to a pile of cupels, and smashed them, and Charlie, a faint irony in his eyes, stepped back to the doorway, out of the way.

Taff methodically smashed every breakable thing in the room, including chair, table, balances, and windows. After he had sledged the iron top of the assay furnace, he took a parting swipe at the stovepipe that brought it down in a crashing shower of soot and ashes.

Throwing the muller into the corner, he surveyed the room, and then his glance shifted to Charlie.

"What's that for?" Charlie asked mildly.

"Does it have to be for anything?" Taff asked wickedly. "Come on. Let's see R. B."

The settlement of Weed was a worked-out placer camp that lay among the gravel buttes on the lower reach of Bone Peak's east slope. In an out-of-the-way back country to begin with, it was remote and almost forgotten, save by a handful of prospectors who touched it twice a summer to replenish their grub from its one sorry store, or by a scattering of riders from the ranches along the Tin Cup that flowed south into more open country. But a man could buy whiskey in Weed, and if he liked whiskey well enough, he could pan for enough gold in the gravel buttes by day to drink whiskey by night, and afterwards take his load to sleep in any one of the score of sagging gray shacks, abandoned and ownerless, that had once been the town. More than one man had learned this, and stayed.

Larkin Moffat had come into Weed in midmorning, with the chill of the Bone Peak crossing still in him, bought himself a drink in the saloon and a bed in the airless bunkroom above it, and slept out the day.

He was awakened sometime after dark by the cackling laugh of a drunken woman below. Over his head he could hear the boards of the roof groaning as they shrank in the night's chill; across the room a man who had come in while Moffat slept groaned in his sleep, and now Moffat was fully awake.

There was, he knew immediately, no reason to get up. He wasn't going anywhere. *Just coming from somewhere again*, he thought wryly. The slate was clean once more.

His thoughts were intolerable; he swung out of his bunk, pulled on his trousers and boots, ran his fingers through his short black hair, put his coat over his arm, and tramped down the stairs into the saloon.

Pausing in the doorway, he looked over the room. It was, he saw, very nearly all things to all men in the town of Weed. There was a short segment of bar near the front entrance which was crowded with men drinking steadily. Directly in front of him and under one of the two over-head kerosene lamps was a circular table at which a poker game was in session. On the shelves immediately to his left were a few bolts of dress goods, and beyond them were sacks of dried fruit and vegetables, an assortment of kegs and barrels, and a meat block, which was a section of a cottonwood stump.

Moffat moved around the poker table to the food. He stuffed his pocket full of soda crackers from a half-filled barrel, picked out a handful of dried jerky from an opened box of it, and then elbowed through the crowd of men to lay a coin on the bar in front of the hard-eyed little man who was tending bar in an oversize dirty apron.

The men were mostly placer miners and prospectors, sun-blackened and ragged and taciturn, indifferent to everything except the whiskey they were paying for out of buckskin pokes of gold dust.

Moffat backed away and moved out on the porch, which was empty. Across the weed-grown road, a prospector had made his campfire. A couple of men were talking to him, and it was here that the drunken woman, seated unsteadily on a packsaddle, was making the night wry with her laughter.

Moffat ate hungrily, watching them. Suddenly, he laughed quietly. These were his people, and he was one of them. *They're all running from something, like I am,* he reflected, and the thought made him feel better.

Tramping down the steps, he went over to the near-by creek with brawled its way over big round boulders and had his drink, afterwards looking at the clear, deep sky. Vermilion was a million miles away. Some night soon, when he had given Charlie Storrs and Josephine time for their visit, he would return. If they had told the camp about him, it was easy enough to drift. If they hadn't, he would stay. Either way, it didn't matter.

Putting on his coat, he tramped back into the saloon, and went directly to the poker table.

"Open game?" he asked.

An unshaven cowman, hat backtilted on his neck, gestured toward a vacant chair and said, "Fresh money. Sure."

Moffat cashed a double eagle and received a generous stack of chips. It was a small-limit game, and he accepted his greasy cards without much enthusiasm.

Packing his pipe, he settled down to an evening of time-killing. It could have been fifteen or twenty hands later when, failing three of a kind on a hand of draw, he threw in his cards, yawned, and looked out over the room.

Dutch Surrency stood at the bar, elbow on it, watching the game. Moffat first felt surprise, and then the old irritation came to him. Dutch nodded to him, and Moffat nodded back. Dutch returned to his drink, and, prodded by one of the players, Moffat anted for the next hand and received his cards.

But his mind was not on the game now. How did Dutch know he was here? Was he after the same old thing? Moffat pondered this for a hand, and then, his defense organized, he cashed in his chips, rose and went over to Dutch.

"Beautiful night," Dutch remarked. He finished his drink, wiped his beard and said, "Let's have a look at it."

He went out onto the porch, and Moffat, hauling up beside him, said flatly, "It's no use, Dutch. Can't you get that through your head?"

"Oh, I know that," Dutch said indifferently. He said no more, only watched the group across the way. The prospector left his friends, walked over to the nearest building, and ripped off a slab from the side of the building. Returning, he stamped the slab into firelengths, stoked the fire, and sat down again.

Moffat said curiously, "How'd you know I'd come here?"

"A freighter from Apex said he never passed you on the road last night. Candace said you didn't take a pack horse. Where else is there?"

Moffat felt the old resentment strong in him, and he asked bluntly, "Then what do you want of me, Dutch?"

"To ask you a couple of things," Dutch said mildly. "First, though, the Corona story is out, Moffat. The whole camp knows it. I picked it up in the Comfort."

Well, that's that, Moffat thought bleakly; Storrs had uncovered him. He waited for Dutch to go on, and when Dutch didn't, Moffat cast back. There had been no censure in Dutch's tone, which was what Moffat was waiting for. Moffat said then, "It's true. Any opinion on the story, Dutch?"

"Parts of it."

"The bribe part?"

"Oh, that. I don't know. At one time in a man's life, money can look too good to him, that's all," Dutch said tranquilly.

There was no censure in this, and Moffat said, "What part, then?"

"The running."

"Could you live with people who knew that about you?" Moffat asked bitterly.

Dutch shrugged, and said nothing, and they were both silent as a man came out of the saloon, paused on the steps, and then, seeing the campfire, staggered drunkenly down the steps and across to it.

Dutch said then, "The thing I wanted to ask you is what you want done with your stuff. Your place is wrecked."

"Wrecked?" Moffat echoed in slow amazement.

"Everything's broken up. No windows, no lock on your door, stuff smashed inside. Candace sent a kid to board it up, but it won't last long."

"Who was it?"

"Taff and a fellow named Storrs, the fellow that knew you. They're telling around they went in to get my assay.

They got it, all right, by figuring back on the papers you'd left around. Then they wrecked the place, figuring you'd drifted."

A slow shame was fired in Moffat then. Their contempt for him was implicit in the act. It would be Charlie Storrs who knew he wouldn't return, because twice before he had run, and Charlie would have heard, just as Josephine would have heard. A miserable and helpless anger was in him when he thought of it.

Dutch said, "I could crate up what's left and send it to you if you knew where you were going, couldn't I?"

From the depths of self-abasement, Moffat answered dismally, "Don't bother with it, Dutch."

"Favor for favor," Dutch said mildly. "You turned me up a fortune. That's little enough to do in return."

That's plain enough, Moffat thought grimly. Favor for favor, purely business, the act of a man who didn't want to owe anybody anything.

And then Dutch said, still tranquilly, "If you decide to change your name after this, be sure and let me know."

A white anger blazed in Moffat. He reached out and fisted Dutch's coat in his hand and yanked him around to face him. "Why would I change my name?" he asked thickly.

"You've run from everything else," Dutch said. "The next thing is to run from your name, isn't it?"

Moffat slowly unfisted his hand and let it fall to his side. Dutch was right, of course; that was the next step, the next hole in which to hide. With a galling bitterness, these past three years ribboned through his memory. There had been just one fact he had faced in those three years, the necessity of changing one hole for another, chased there by the ghost of his dishonesty. Once he had almost killed a man for remarking his connection with Corona. The second time was worse; he had been dismissed from a responsible position by the mine superintendent, the memory of whose icy contempt at learning his identity still made him wince with shame.

And now, when he had forsaken pride and his work, had abjured ambition and money, his past had caught up with him again. His shop was wrecked, his shame laid bare, and he had accepted it—but running. *To Weed*, he

40

thought contemptuously, *or to change my name and hide behind a new one, like Dutch said.*

He waited a moment for acceptance to come, as it had come in the past. Instead, he felt only anger that was stronger than disgust. It was an indiscriminate anger, at himself and at Charlie Storrs and Bill Taff, at his own stubborn pride that demanded respect where respect was not due. He thought with a gray distaste, *How far can you run?* and finally answered himself, *No farther than this.* He let himself think for a moment of what his return would be like, and he did not like it, and he thought grimly, *That's your pride.*

A moment afterward, he spoke in a voice that held no humility. "Dutch, did you find a foreman?"

"I—think so," Dutch answered hesitatingly.

Moffat looked sharply at him. "Let him go," he said harshly. "Who is he?"

Dutch answered dryly, "Why, Larkin Moffat, you fool."

Without another word Moffat wheeled, and tramped into the saloon, after his saddle and his few possessions abovestairs.

The trail from Weed traveled a succession of lowering, timbered valleys until it picked up the bigger Valley of the Bone, where it followed the creek until the road, across the creek, passed over a bridge, and trail and road joined a mile below town. They had picked up the road when they heard the noon whistle from the stamp mill. Its shrill echo lingered between the peaks a moment, and died.

When they reached the main street, Surrency said, "Candace can scrape up dinner for us. Come along, Larkin."

Moffat thanked him, but refused, promising to meet him later, and they parted in the traffic at the four corners. As he moved off Dutch looked over his shoulder, about to speak. His words died and only the look in his eyes, one of concern, remained. He waved carelessly and Moffat sat his horse until Dutch took the hill alongside the Comfort and vanished.

A scattering of millhands was straggling down the hill, and Moffat dismounted stiffly and tied his horse to the hotel tie rail. He had pondered the manner and order of his return, and, having it in mind, he cut up the hill alongside the hotel and, below the meat market, he crossed the road. He spoke idly to a pair of millhands and then stepped into the open door of Jarboe's office.

There was a man sitting in the swivel chair in front of the desk, a roughly dressed, barrel of a man whose full mustache was a lighter color than the skin of his ruddy face. He was whittling delicately, paying close attention to it, as Moffat entered.

Now he brushed the fine shavings from his lap, closed his knife, laid it on the desk, and said, "What can I do for you, my friend?"

"Bill Taff around?" Moffat asked, sauntering into the room. The light was behind him, and he saw the man peering closely at him, a growing suspicion climbing into his eyes, the certainty not yet there.

"You're—" That was all he got out, when Moffat lunged. The man came out of his chair with a leap, but Moffat's momentum was already established. They met with a grunt, and the drive of Moffat's shoulder carried the squat man back against the desk. Pinning him, Moffat fumbled at the man's belt. A long overhand blow caught him on the cheek, hurting, and Moffat saw the man had picked up the closed knife and, with two inches of it sticking from his fist, was trying for Moffat's eyes. The second blow he ducked, taking it on the neck, and now he had the man's gun.

He fell away then, putting his whole weight into it, holding the man's belt as he moved. The man was swung in a wide half-circle, and Moffat let go and saw him sprawl across the floor and crash against the legs of the table.

Both table legs broke, and the magazines and ore samples which cluttered it cascaded down on him.

He scrambled to his feet, arms widespread, the closed knife still in his hand, his eyes hot with anger and little caution in them.

Moffat hefted the man's gun and asked, "Know who I am?"

"I got an idea."

"Get out. Go tell Taff and Jarboe."

42

The man backed out the door and stood in the path a moment, watching. Moffat turned to the desk and pulled out all the drawers, pitching them upside down on the floor. All the papers that lay on the counter he brushed off onto the floor, too, and he looked up and saw the man still watching him. Slowly, he raised the pistol and cocked it; as he lowered it, the man ducked and vanished.

Moffat let the gun off cock and pitched it in the corner and went about his work. He overturned the desk on its face, then, picking up the swivel chair, he crashed it down on the back of the desk. When there was so little of the chair left that it had no sledging weight, and the desk was splintered, he cast the fragments of the chair aside and looked outside again. A trio of curious millhands, attracted by the racket, had stopped to watch.

Moffat picked up the lone straightback chair and threw it through the window. The millhands hurried on. Looking about him, Moffat saw the only remaining thing undamaged was the safe. He pulled his gun and holding it close to the safe dial, fired twice. The dial bent, but did not break off. It was enough, and Moffat looked around him as he slipped two fresh loads into his gun. He saw the spittoon then and put a hole through it.

There was nothing more to wreck and, short of setting the building on fire, no more damage to accomplish. It wasn't much, he reflected, *But Jarboe will get the idea*.

Stepping out into the road, he found he had collected a handful of curious spectators who stood at a respectful distance in front of Caslin's Meat Market. That was good, too, since this was in the open now.

He cut angling across the road to the corner of the hotel and, mounting the steps, went in. The lobby held groups of men talking, and ahead of him Moffat saw five of the camp's mine owners in conversation. Three of them, Hazeltine, Bishop, and Murphy, had sent assay work to him, and, skirting the group, he nodded to them. Murphy glanced quickly away; Hazeltine found the wall behind Moffat of consuming interest, and Bishop stared at him stonily. Moffat felt a slow flush mounting to his face, and he thought grimly, *I can get used to that, too*.

He moved on to the desk where Mrs. Barber, harried and massive, was scolding somebody through the door

43

under the stairs that opened onto the dining room. She turned, and saw Moffat, and said bluntly, "Yes?" and then, "Oh, hello, Moffat."

"Have you got a Charlie Storrs here, Mrs. Barber?"

Mrs. Barber knew. She said warningly, "No trouble here, Moffat. Take it outside. Besides, he isn't here."

She looked beyond him then to the lobby and said, dryly, "There's his fine wife, though; just came down for her breakfast."

Moffat felt something tighten within him, felt his face smooth into a stubborn set. This was part of it, though, and he must go through with it. Slowly, he took a deep breath, said, "Thank you," and turned and looked over the lobby.

Josephine had seen him, was watching him. She raised a hand and wiggled her fingers, remaining seated. Moffat walked woodenly across the lobby, removing his hat as he approached. This was the moment he had been afraid of, along with the other; but seeing Josephine, the warm and teasing welcome in her smile, he felt nothing except an obscure guilt. But three years had dulled it, and he halted and said without much effort, "How are you, Josephine?"

Josephine Storrs read a humor into this meeting, he saw. She said dryly, "It used to be worth a kiss, Larkin. Much less time used to be worth a kiss."

Moffat said, "Only in front of Charlie, now," and when she put out her hand he took it.

She pulled him into the chair beside her, and looked at him frankly, her blue eyes tender with memory, going over each detail of his face. He submitted, holding her glance, and a part of him was thinking, *She was yours for the asking, once.*

She said, then, "Charlie said you wouldn't be back."

"Charlie isn't always right," Moffat murmured.

"How long has it been?"

Moffat answered steadily, "Since I was kicked out of Corona, three years lacking a month. Since I saw you last, three years."

"Ah, Larkin," Josephine said softly. "You never understood that I didn't care what you did. How could you go, and without me?"

The corner of Moffat's mouth curled in a wry smile. "It takes a man a lifetime to learn some things, Josephine."

She looked searchingly at him and turned her head away, and Moffat sat there motionless, reaching back for that time, and wondering why he had done what he did, then, and afterwards.

"And how has the world treated you, Larkin?" Josephine asked lightly.

"I haven't looked at it much," Moffat murmured, and it was almost to himself.

Josephine glanced at him quizzically, and now it was Moffat's turn to have his full look at her. She was slim, in a dark suit that held the quiet elegance of good living. A faint scent of verbena clung to her, and her hair, black as an Indian's but fine as cobweb, was done in a strange and careful city fashion that was admirable and foreign to him. Only the mouth, a tiny cleft at each corner of it that gave the fleeting illusion of a pout, had changed; and Moffat, thinking of Charlie Storrs, accepted the fact with charity.

"I've looked at a lot of it," Josephine said. She waited until he was looking in her eyes, and then asked, "Did you know about us—Charlie and me?"

Moffat nodded, said, "For whatever they are worth, you have my well wishes."

"I would rather have had something else," Josephine said, watching him.

Moffat stirred uncomfortably, and at that moment he heard the sharp, drawling command that overrode the subdued clamor of the room.

"Stand up, Moffat!"

3

MOFFAT knew who had spoken. Even before he turned he had a moment of fleeting regret that Taff had braced him here, where the presence of Josephine barred gunplay.

He rose slowly, wheeled slowly, and saw Taff by the open door. The man he had just pitched out of Jarboe's was deeper into the lobby, and beside him was a small, older man, and it was this man who held the gun on him.

45

Standing in the doorway was Charlie Storrs, and now Moffat looked at Taff indolently, and then shifted his gaze to Storrs.

"Hello, Charlie," Moffat said. "Are you in this, or are you just tagging along?"

Storrs said sharply, "Josephine, go upstairs!"

Moffat did not hear Josephine move, and now Taff said, "Get his gun, Max."

The man he had pitched out of Jarboe's came forward, careful to keep from placing himself between Moffat and the man who held the gun.

He took Moffat's gun, and said to Josephine, "Better move, lady," and backed away.

Josephine said in a low voice, "Shall I, Larkin?"

"Yes," Moffat said and he sized this up and did not like it. The men who had been in the lobby edged toward the dining room, and some of the diners were filling the doorway to watch the show. It would be a beating, Moffat knew, Max and Bill Taff administering it while the man with the gun stood off any interference. And nobody except Josephine would be sorry about it.

Bill Taff came forward, and Mrs. Barber's angry voice cut across the lobby. "Bill Taff, you take your fight outside!"

"Shut up, Fatty," Taff said mildly. "He won't fight. He'll run."

Max began to move in too, and Moffat heard Josephine retreat across the lobby; he was watching Taff, measuring the hulk of the wide shoulders, the square face that was smiling wickedly in anticipation. It was Taff he'd have to lick, and he began to shuck off his coat.

Max lunged then, hoping to catch him with his arms tangled in coat sleeves; he rushed ponderously, head down, arms outspread.

Moffat stepped aside and as Max overshot him, he brought his forearm down viciously across the man's heavy neck. Max crashed headlong into the chair Josephine had been sitting in, and now Moffat quickly shed his coat, throwing it aside and moving out into the room.

Taff was still coming, and he said, "You did all right on Arnie with a chunk of rock, Moffat, but I don't think you're good."

46

"But you won't take a chance on it, will you?" Moffat taunted.

Taff waited until Max had come off the floor, and Max, without instruction, circled wide, and when he was quartering on Moffat from another direction Taff said, "All right," and came on.

Moffat was near the wall; he stepped back, letting the wall cover his back. Taff reached him first, and Moffat moved into him, grappling, and trying to wheel him in between himself and Max.

Taff understood his intent, and he wrapped his long arms around Moffat's midriff and lifted, so that Moffat's leverage was gone. Max hit him quartering with the whole weight of his burly body, his shoulder point first, and the breath was driven from Moffat's body. The impact half turned Taff around, and Moffat sank his hand in Taff's tow hair and bent his head back and raked an elbow roughly across Taff's face. At the same moment, he felt a smashing blow in the kidneys from Max that paralyzed him. Taff's hold relaxed, and because Moffat's legs would not hold him for the moment, he fell to his knees.

Max was already charging again, and Moffat, falling in front of him, tripped him. Max staggered and caromed into Taff, and crashed headlong across Moffat's legs; Moffat, pulling clear and rolling away, kicked viciously at Max's face and connected and tried to come up. His legs did not quite have his weight when Taff was in, sledging great wide swings at his face. One blow caught him on the ear, and Taff followed through with the whole weight of his body, lunging.

Moffat's back and head crashed into the wall with a violence that sent a blazing pinwheel of stars before his eyes, and he thought, falling, *It'll come now*.

Then he heard above the rasping breath of Taff the single inexplicable gunshot, and felt Taff's smashing blow on his cheek. He rolled violently, in panic, and felt Taff lose him, and he lunged to his feet, looking around for Max. And then he saw Surrency.

Dutch had a gun in the back of Taff's disarmed watchdog. In the other hand he held a six-gun, too, pointed at the ceiling.

Max was dragging himself to his feet, and Dutch

47

booted his rump with savage kicks that sent him sprawling.

Taff was on his knees, against the wall, and Dutch waited until Taff slowly came to his feet, and then he said, "Let's make it even, Bill."

Taff said, "Any time, any time," and he rubbed a sleeve across his bloody nose, and did not look at Moffat.

Max picked himself up, and glanced wickedly at Dutch, and Dutch said, "You go sit down, and stay there."

Max began to back away, and now, for the first time, Dutch looked at Moffat.

"All right," Dutch said, "take him."

"The only thing he can take is a bribe," Taff jibed.

For the first time, hope came to Moffat, and with it the anger, feral and unreasoning, and for the first time in three years, washed clean of guilt.

He moved toward Taff, and Taff shoved away from the wall and faced him, fisted hands crossed belt-high. Moffat came at him, and there was in him the desire to maim and kill, and he slashed a driving blow at Taff's face, and Taff hit him in the belly. For perhaps ten seconds, they stood toe to toe, slugging massively, and then Taff, flinching against the hurt of it, gave way a step. Moffat moved in by instinct, then, seeing only Taff's bleeding face; and now he struck at the blood and he felt Taff's nose mash under the blow that raked cheek and ear and would have fallen across Taff's shoulder if he had stood.

But Taff went down, skidding across the rough floor until he was brought up against the door frame, and Moffat stalked him. A sleeve hung from Moffat's elbow; he ripped it off as Taff scrambled wearily to his feet, and Moffat hit him again, this time in the belly, and again, doggedly, in the belly. Taff folded his arms across his belly then, and Moffat hit him in the face, driving him back through the doorway.

Taff spread his arms to grab the door frame, but he was seconds late, already falling backwards down the steps. He turned a complete somersault on the steps and landed on his back with a jar that shook the last breath from him, and Moffat, coming down the steps, could not wait. His lunge at Taff, who was rolling to his knees, missed the last three steps, and he landed astradle Taff's chest and slashed once at Taff's face before they rolled together under the tie rail and out into the mud.

Taff fought with panic, not striking, struggling only to get Moffat clear of him, and they came up together. Moffat hit him again, doggedly, with no care or caution for himself, and Taff pawed weakly at him, more of a push than a blow. Taff's face, an agony seared into it, told the silent watchers who had trailed them through the door and down the steps that he had enough.

And still Moffat came on. At each sullen, vicious blow, Taff backed up, unfisted hands swinging aimlessly, words forming and bubbling from his broken lips, and no sound coming. And now he stepped back into the pool of thin, red mud before the Comfort, his feet making slow waves as he moved, always backwards, deeper.

And Moffat came on, dragging his feet, hitting out wickedly, slowly, viciously; he waded into the water, too, not noticing and past caring. He slipped and fell to his knees in the maroon mud, and Taff, sensing the end, sat down. Moffat came off his knees in a half-crouch, too tired to rise, and when he reached Taff, he hit him again, this time in the face. Taff rolled over backwards, sending a great cascade of thin maroon mud into the air, and Moffat crawled astride him, and as the mud washed back over Taff's face, he slugged doggedly, his blows sliding off Taff's face, sending streamers of muck into the air.

At the gathering murmur of protest from the crowd, a couple of miners moved in and stopped it. They pulled Moffat off Taff, and stood him on his feet, and he drunkenly swung at them. Two more men moved in and pulled Taff into a sitting position. He was formless, inert, a sodden lump of flesh underneath the red muck that covered every part of him.

Moffat ceased struggling. The two men let go of his arms, and he promptly sat down, and they pulled him to his feet again.

Slowly, breathing deeply, he looked about him, as if trying to remember where he was. Dutch stood at the edge of the pool, alone now, watching him. Behind Dutch, Moffat saw Charlie Storrs on the hotel steps, and he wondered tiredly what it was he had wanted to say to Storrs. Beyond Charlie, in the lobby doorway, Josephine stood, and Moffat, with a vast effort of will, concentrated his gaze on Dutch.

Dutch said mildly, "Well, you've planted your flag, Larkin."

Candace was a quarter-mile down the Big Jay's haul road when she met the first miners coming off the noon shift, beginning their three-mile trek to town for supper. They politely took the cliff edge while she crowded the buggy against the bank of the dug road. Their pale faces that seldom saw enough sunlight, looked gray and exhausted as she passed them; a few knew her and spoke, the rest plodded past in weary silence.

Now, just below the Big Jay, she came into the day's last sunlight. Far beneath her, the timbered Valley of the Bone lay in evening dusk, while the sun itself seemed balanced on the very peaks of the Vermilions across the valley.

She could hear the racket of hammers and axes. As she rounded the last bend and the Big Jay was in sight, she saw the timberers at work. The log buildings of the Big Jay were clustered tightly on the narrow shelf of land in front of the tunnel mouth; on the lip of the shelf was the big log orebin and below it the road where the ore wagons usually loaded. But now a crew was at work here, and the timbers and frame of a long, steeply slanting ore chute were already stretching from the bin and angling down the hill and crossing a steep wash to Dacy's adjoining claim. This, Candace knew, was the measure her father was using to move the ore off Big Jay property where Jarboe could not seize it, and where he could store it until it was moved to a mill in Apex. She remembered it had been Moffat's idea, and she thought about him, recalling everything her father had told her of his visit to Weed, and of Moffat's beating of Bill Taff. How much of the cause of the fight lay in Taff's wrecking Moffat's shack, and how much lay in the man's wild protest against the guilt in his past? She didn't know, and she speculated on what he would be like, now that he was carrying no secret and had put shame behind him. *Or has he?* she wondered, and she knew she understood nothing about this man save what she had second-hand from her father—and that was not enough.

50

She passed the loading road and climbed the tunnel road and presently put her buggy down the tight lane that separated the log office from the huge and unused commissary and bunkhouse across the way. Reining in, she climbed out of the buggy and tied her horse, afterwards lifting out the lunch basket.

Black smoke was lifting from the boiler house beside the hoist shack, and she could hear the clanging of the gears as the car lifted up the shaft. A couple of muckers, come to the tunnel mouth for a breather, touched their hats to her and disappeared down the tunnel. She could see the small pinpoint flames of their candles at the shaft head down the tunnel, and she turned into the office.

It was a bare room, with the unused assay office opening off to the left. A couple of flat desks, a bookkeeper's desk and stool, a stove and assortment of chairs made up the furniture. She saw the litter of pipe ashes on the floor and wished for a broom.

Putting her basket on one of the tables, she went to a door in the right wall and gently opened it. In the small cubbyhole of a room which was Larkin Moffat's quarters, she saw her father sleeping on the bunk.

Candace closed the door softly, and was taking off her shawl when the outer door opened, and Larkin Moffat stepped in.

Candace hadn't seen him since the night he left for Weed; she smiled uncertainly and said, "You must be hungry. It's just six."

Moffat closed the door with his bandaged hand, and tossed his spiked candlestick on the table. He was roughly dressed in stained corduroy, and the bandage on his hand was soiled. The smile he gave her stopped halfway to end in a wince. His right cheekbone held a purple bruise as big as a silver dollar, and there was a cut on his other cheek. One corner of his mouth was tightly swollen, and it gave him an appearance of mock gravity that the friendliness in his eyes belied. He was bigger than she remembered, and somehow relaxed and easy.

He said, "I was never hungrier," and then added morosely, "But can I eat? I couldn't this morning."

"I'll cut up everything in small pieces."

Moffat grimaced, and then tried another smile. "Dutch asleep?"

Candace nodded. "Let's let him be. He can eat anytime."

Candace turned to the lunch basket, thinking, *He's changed,* and unable to to pin down exactly in what way. Maybe it was his easy acceptance of her now. She had boned a roast grouse for Moffat and her father, and there were cold roast potatoes, fresh bread and chokecherry jelly, and a whole dried apple pie.

She spread it out on the table and Moffat groaned in anticipation. Smiling, Candace sat down, and Moffat half sat on the edge of the table. He broke a breast of his grouse and extended her half, which she took, and he began to eat.

She took a shred of the grouse meat and put the rest beside him and watched him eat hungrily. The wryness she had felt in him before, the deep corroding indifference, was gone and in its place was the contentedness of a man pleasurably at work, she thought.

"How's the job?" she asked then.

Moffat spoke around his food. "The chute will be done when the midnight shift comes on. Then we'll move ore."

"You like this, don't you?" Candace asked curiously.

Moffat stopped chewing and looked levelly at her. "Better than anything."

"Better than assay work?" Candace asked slyly.

Moffat grimaced. "A cook's job." He looked full at her, then, and shook his head. "You had a rough tongue that night."

"But not rough enough. It didn't get me what I wanted."

Moffat shrugged. "I'm here."

"You got yourself here, I didn't," Candace said.

She saw his face alter subtly into thoughtfulness, and she wondered if she had said too much. His change of heart was none of her business, she knew, and she watched anxiously as he slowly laid the grouse down and wiped his fingers on the napkin.

"It took me long enough," he said at last, and then he looked at her, surprising her watching him.

She said, "That doesn't count now, does it?" in a gentle voice.

"No," Moffat answered slowly, "Only to myself."

"And that's a mistake, too."

Moffat was reaching for the bread. His hand paused and he looked searchingly at her. "How's that?"

"Never look back," Candace said. "Remember Lot's wife?"

"Not the same thing."

Candace was silent a second, hesitating, and then she said, "There's another way of putting it."

Moffat was watching her.

"Pity anything but yourself," Candace said.

Moffat held her glance a long moment, and then looked down at the food. He looked at this a long moment, too, as if trying to remember what it was he had intended eating. Then he said. "That's something to remember. I'm sorry." Suddenly, he glanced up at her, and said, "Now don't say, 'You are, like hell.'"

Candace really laughed then, and Moffat, smiling, watched her.

Candace said, "I like you better this way, with just a little salt on. Not too much, like before."

"Now who's looking back?" Moffat countered.

"That's my privilege, not yours."

Moffat grinned and reached in the basket for the pie. He lifted it out onto the table, and was poking around the basket for a knife to cut it with when the door opened.

Moffat turned, and Candace did too. The first person to come through the door was Josephine Storrs. Charlie Storrs followed her and closed the door.

"Good evening, Miss Surrency," he said, and he bowed slightly to Candace. "Good evening, Larkin."

Candace nodded. Moffat said, "You keep odd hours at your job, Charlie." He remembered Candace then, and introduced her to Josephine.

Then Charlie Storrs said matter-of-factly, "I came on business, Larkin. But before we discuss it I want to tell you I resent that remark you made in the hotel yesterday. Since when have I tagged along with three men to watch them beat up another man?"

Candace glanced at Moffat. She saw his jaw set faintly, and then it relaxed, and he contrived a suggestion of a smile. "You're right, Charlie. I apologize."

Charlie Storrs smiled affably then. "I think you had other things on your mind."

"I did," Moffat said. "One of them was how to face a town after the story you told."

"Did I lie about anything?" Charlie asked.

Moffat shook his head and smiled thinly. "Not one damn thing, Charlie. That's what made it so hard."

Josephine said, "You know, I could close my eyes, and you two take me back four years. Have you ever met each other without arguing?" She laughed then, and said to Candace, "It can get tiresome after so much of it."

Moffat said gently, "Can't it," and turned to drag up some chairs. Josephine thanked him and sat down.

Moffat put his leg up on the table again, and picked up the knife and cut the pie. He poised the knife and said, "Will anybody join me in a piece of pie, or can I have it myself, like I want?"

Charlie smiled dryly and said, "No, go ahead."

Both Candace and Josephine demurred, and Candace watched Moffat cut the pie, thinking, *You've won, Larkin Moffat. You can fight it with reason, now, and not your fists. Nobody can hurt you very much now.*

She felt an unreasoning pride in him then that she hugged to herself. Moffat cut a wedge of pie, picked it up in his fingers, and began unconcernedly to eat.

He swallowed the first bite and said, "Come up to look over the Big Jay, Charlie?"

"That's right," Charlie said pleasantly. "You know, legally you can't keep me out. The lessor—"

"Go ahead," Moffat said indifferently.

Charlie said, "You won't try to stop me? I thought since you were keeping the assay a secret, you'd make trouble on everything else."

Moffat looked directly at him. "We've no secrets from you, Charlie. Especially the assay."

Charlie Storrs's broad face colored under Moffat's gaze. Charlie inclined his head. "Score one for you, my friend."

He drew a paper from his pocket and tossed it on the table. "Jarboe's written permission for me to examine the property."

Moffat didn't pick it up, but merely went on eating his pie.

Charlie looked at Candace now. "Would you mind if Josephine stayed here? I don't think she'd enjoy the mine much."

"Not at all," Candace said.

Charlie said to Moffat then, "I'll try to keep out of the way."

"I'll help you," Moffat said. He rose, wiping his hands on his mud-caked trousers.

"Don't bother yourself," Charlie said.

"No bother. No trouble. In fact, it's a necessity, Charlie. I'm going to peek over your shoulder."

Charlie smiled unpleasantly, "I don't see what harm I could do your lease, but then if you don't trust me—" He shrugged.

"Now why should I?" Moffat asked gently.

Charlie closed his mouth in a grim line and was silent. Moffat reached in a box under the table for a couple of candlesticks. This seemed to remind him of the growing dusk, for he moved over and lighted the lamp in the wall bracket. Then he motioned Charlie toward the door, smiled to Candace and Josephine, and went out.

Alone with Josephine now, Candace rose and went over to the table and the lunch basket.

Josephine said dryly, "They're always like that. They always have been, ever since I've known them."

There was no comment Candace could make on this, but because she wanted to be pleasant, she asked, "And how long has that been?"

"Larkin five years and Charlie four," Josephine replied. "And I think most of the arguments start because of Charlie. This one did, anyway."

Candace was putting away the pie in the basket, and she said, "Because of what he told about Larkin?"

"Yes. That's unforgivable."

"I don't agree with you," Candace said, and now she looked at Josephine. "Somebody had to do it. Why not your husband?"

Josephine regarded her coolly, and then raised her eyebrows. *"Had* to do it? Does anyone *have* to make someone else miserable? Can't a man make a mistake without having it haunt him all his life?"

Candace didn't look up from her tidying up. "That's the trouble. It haunted him too long. Now it doesn't, since it's in the open."

She looked up in time to see Josephine regarding her with a cold and calculated interest. She was suddenly aware of her plain dress, of the kind of careless disarray in which a day's work always left her. Josephine, she admitted, was pretty and scrubbed-looking and immaculate and pleasant enough, but Candace was aware of both a condescension and a pity in her manner, and she resented it. She was at a disadvantage in discussing Moffat, she knew, for Josephine had known him, and she did not.

Josephine, as if reading her mind, asked, "How long have you known Larkin?"

"Not at all. I've talked with him twice."

"He's had a bad time."

"Yes. It must have been."

"He's lost other jobs since it happened, you know."

Candace said she didn't know; she found herself listening intently and wondered why.

"He almost killed a man in Nevada for telling about the Corona dismissal. That's why I came along tonight. I thought he might fight Charlie."

Candace said mildly, "I don't think you need to worry about that any more."

"You don't know Larkin," Josephine said smugly.

"That well, I do."

"But not as well as I do," Josephine said insistently.

Candace looked levelly at her. "That's what you keep saying. How well did you know him?"

Josephine shrugged, and said with a quiet malice that was overlaid with sweetness, "You can figure it out for yourself. He asked me to marry him."

Candace pulled the cloth over the basket, and now she was thinking angrily, *All right. You asked for it, didn't you?* And then she said, with a voice that matched Josephine's in sweetness, "Surely that must have been after you were already married."

The two women looked at each other, their dislike of each other not even hidden now, and Candace thought angrily, *I can swing a tomahawk, too, Puss.* When Josephine didn't speak, Candace turned back to her work.

Waiting deep in the tunnel for the cage at the head of the shaft, Charlie Storrs teetered unconcernedly on his heels, aware that Moffat, the point of his shoulder against the wall, was watching him. The cage came up, and they waited for the two muckers to move the ore cars off down the track, and then they stepped on the platform and began the descent. Charlie, who had carefully made notes on the condition of the equipment and machinery on top, said, "Can't say much for the condition of your equipment."

"That's Jarboe," Moffat murmured. "It was probably third-hand when he got it."

Charlie grinned in what was meant to be friendly understanding, but Moffat's face remained sober, and Charlie looked away.

The cage stopped at the second and lower level, and Moffat, holding his lighted candle, led the way down the drift. The track on which the ore cars were hauled was centered in the drift. Mules, urged on by the curses of the trammers, hauled the ore cars past them at intervals on their way to the hoist. Moffat spoke to the trammers and moved on through pools of seeping water, paying no attention to Charlie.

Twice Charlie stopped and stabbed his candlestick into timbers and inspected the cribbing and timbering; each time Moffat waited for him.

Finally, they came to the stoping of the pocket where Dutch's ore lay. The cavernous room, lighted only by the candles of the miners, spiked in the wall, seemed aswarm with noise and men. At the head were three single jackers, filling the stope with the din of their sledges as they drilled. A pair of muckers labored steadily and mightily at loading the cars with ore. A brace of timbermen were shaping stulls out of the way of the others. The candlelight, dim as it was, picked out a million facets of glittering silver in the ore at the breast, and Charlie looked at it with undisguised envy.

Moffat said dryly, "You won't be buying this," and touched his arm to move him out of the way of the trammers.

He pointed down the dark drift. "There's what you want."

Down the drift lay the old working head that had been abandoned when Dutch found the pocket. Charlie only nodded and said, "This'll take time. I want to mark out some ore for mill tests."

Moffat said coldly, "How much?"

"Five. A couple on the first level, three here. Two ton each, let's say."

"Let's don't," Moffat said. "Ten tons. How'll you move it?"

"The same way you are."

Moffat shook his head. "This mine is leased with all its equipment, Charlie. That means tracks, cars, hoist, and machinery, working twenty-four hours a day. If you put any men down here and they get in my way, I'll run over 'em. I'm not moving any ore for Jarboe."

Charlie scowled, the candlelight touching his broad face in a way that deepened its lines and exaggerated its expressiveness.

"Hell," he snorted, "if I can't move ore, how can I test?"

"That's hard to figure," Moffat agreed.

"Then letting me in doesn't mean a damned thing?"

"I guess that's it."

Charlie stood motionless, baffled and angry, a hot belligerence in his face. "Then if I want a test, I'll have to wait until your lease is up?"

"Unless you can get ore out without getting in my way, that's right."

Charlie was silent a moment, glaring at him, and Moffat thought, *Five years ago he'd have fought. He's learning too.*

Charlie shrugged, then. "Well, damned if I'll send back a recommendation to buy a property and put in a mill on the results of an assay of a forty-pound sample."

"Suit yourself."

"Let's go."

They were almost past the stope when Moffat was hailed from the face by a big, huge-boned and towering man. Moffat paused and waited for Adam Lloyd, his head driller, to cross the stope. He handed Moffat a pair of dull drills to deliver to the blacksmith on top, and afterward Moffat fell in beside Charlie and they silently made their way back to the hoist.

On top again, Moffat dropped off the drills at the blacksmith shop next to the stables. Charlie, meanwhile, his candle whipped out by the steady insistent breeze, followed the track out to the ore bin, and Moffat saw him silhouetted against the night sky. He went over to him, and by this time Charlie had climbed along the timber of the overflowing ore bin and was peering down the slope into the night. The racket of the crew working by lanternlight on the chute came fitfully to Moffat as he waited for Charlie to have his look.

When Charlie returned, he said, "I meant to ask you. What are you doing that for?"

"To get the ore off Jarboe's property."

"Why not mill it?"

"It's Jarboe's mill," Moffat said dryly.

Charlie only laughed, and headed back for the office and Moffat fell in beside him.

As soon as they entered the office, Moffat saw something was wrong. Josephine rose immediately, and nodded to Candace and said, "Good night." She turned to Charlie, with scarcely a look at Moffat, and said, "Can't we go, Charlie?"

Storrs said they could; he bowed to Candace, gave Moffat a pleasant enough good night, and stood aside while Josephine went out into the night.

Charlie assisted Josephine into the rig, pulled the blanket over her lap, untied the team, and climbed up beside her.

They took the haul road in silence, and then Josephine asked idly, "Get what you wanted?"

Charlie chuckled. "No, and I knew I wouldn't. I didn't even get Larkin mad enough to fight."

"I wouldn't try if I were you," Josephine said. "He'd hurt you. Remember Bill Taff?"

"I take some killing too," Charlie said comfortably. "Enjoy your visit?"

Josephine, remembering, looked straight ahead and said, "That little fluff is after Larkin."

"They pair off nicely," Charlie observed. "Give them three years and Larkin will have a greasy beard, he'll chew tobacco with his meals, and she'll be sewing him up in his underwear in the fall, just like any Cousin Jack."

"She's pretty," Josephine said grudgingly.

"So are some Indian girls," Charlie said carelessly. "Still, if you like her, you better get acquainted. We're here till Surrency's lease is up."

Josephine looked at him. "Why?"

Charlie told of Moffat's refusal to allow him time and facilities to move ore for the necessary assays. He finished by saying, "Now don't yell about it. You can go back to San Francisco anytime you want—only I've got to stay."

Josephine said calmly, "I'll stay."

Charlie glanced obliquely at her, puzzled. "You've changed your tune."

"If you can stand it, I can," Josephine said placidly.

Charlie snorted. "That's the first time I've ever seen you resigned to anything, except the fact you're a woman."

"A pretty one, too, am I not?"

Charlie grinned. "That gets no argument from me."

Charlie let Josephine off at the hotel, and returned the rented rig to Paxton's stable. He was hungry again, but not hungry enough to face the food he knew he would get at the restaurant on the side street. Standing in the driveway of the stable, he lighted a cigar and looked over the town, a feeling of restlessness in him. The dying road held some traffic, and there was a scattering of horses tied in front of the Comfort. The infernal din from the Silverbell's piano had started up again; he took the road, heading for the corner, wondering if the racket would keep him awake tonight, wondering too if it would rain.

At the four corners, he looked idly up the street toward the stamp mill. Seeing a shaft of light issuing from Jarboe's office, he turned up the hill, and presently halted in Jarboe's doorway.

His first feeling was one of surprise. Everything in the office was new, and it was arranged differently. Where the desk had once sat was an armchair, and a man was seated in it. Against the wall to the left was a new rolltop desk with matching chair.

Jarboe sat in the new swivel chair, and he had swung it around so that it faced his companion. But the thing Charlie's glance lingered on was the huge new brass cuspidor alongside Jarboe's chair.

Charlie stepped in, asking genially, "Open for business?" and then his glance settled on Jarboe's companion. For a moment Charlie didn't recognize him. It was Bill Taff, he saw.

Taff's face was almost unrecognizable; both cheeks were bruised black, his lips great sausages, and his nose was vastly swollen and purple and shapeless. Charlie clucked sympathetically. "Man, man, you ought to be in bed."

"I'm all right," Taff said surlily.

Jarboe said, "Did you get past the office at the Big Jay?"

"Barely."

"What's he got, a pocket?"

"A big one, as far as I could tell."

"Is he robbing?"

Charlie scowled. "He's gutting it. Who wouldn't? But he's timbering and cribbing and taking some care."

"How much ore has he moved?"

Charlie made a guess, and Jarboe scowled. Then Charlie told him of Moffat's refusal to allow him to bring out ore for an assay. He also told him of the ore chute Moffat was completing to the dump on the adjoining claim.

"Chute?" Jarboe interrupted. "Chute to where?"

"Dacy's claim, if I remember the plat."

"I remember," Jarboe said. "How long?"

"Hundred and fifty feet to the other side of that wash."

Jarboe scratched his scalp thoughtfully. "He must have trestled that wash. He better hope he don't get a good rain." He looked mildly, thoughtfully, at Bill Taff, who merely shifted in his chair.

"Well, well," Jarboe said then, apropos of nothing, and continued, "Well, well, well."

Charlie said, "This cools off our deal for a while, Jarboe."

"It does. You leaving?"

Charlie shook his head in negation. "No. I'm going to look over the other four claims and the Enricher mine. If it looks like we could do business with the others, I'll make assays and surveys. I'll still be around when Dutch's lease is up."

Jarboe only nodded, and now Charlie yawned and said, "I'm off to bed. Good night, both of you."

He went out, and Jarboe watched the empty doorway for the space of a full minute. Then from his pocket he drew out a new plug of tobacco and a knife. He opened the knife, cut a corner from the plug, put it in his mouth, carefully licked both sides of the knife blade to clean it, closed the knife, and returned both knife and tobacco to his pocket. Taff watched him until he was finished, and then observed, "Sounds like you're getting poorer by the hour."

Jarboe didn't comment. He shifted the tobacco around in his mouth until he had it placed satisfactorily, and then he asked, "How you feeling?" with a dry concern.

Taff said immediately. "Not very good."

Jarboe leaned over and spat, then said, "Well, he's a pretty big man."

Taff came forward in his chair, his battered face sulky. "Look, R. B. I'm not scared of him. I'm not scared of any man that walks. Only, when he comes after me, I at least want to have a finger that'll go inside a trigger guard." He held up his hands, which were bruised and swollen until the fingers stood straight out from the palms.

"But I'm getting poorer every hour. You said so."

"You won't get any richer roughing him up. He don't rough."

"But he's moving ore," Jarboe said gently.

Taff scowled and crossed his legs, groaning a little at the exertion. He looked at his boots and said, "You're going at it wrong, R. B."

"How's that?"

"Fight him with something he hasn't got and you have."

Jarboe smiled faintly. "Brains, you mean?"

"Money."

Moffat came awake to someone shaking him gently. He opened his eyes and saw the hulking figure of Adam Lloyd, his head driller, standing beside his bunk in the half-light of early morning. Moffat had gone to bed after the midnight shift came on; he was still sleepy, but wide enough awake to realize Lloyd's visit was important, and now he rolled over and yawned.

"Don't you ever sleep, Adam?" he growled.

Adam said, "It's half-past six, Larkin, and only one of the shift has showed up for work." He shook his head, forebodingly. "Where they at?"

Wordlessly, Moffat climbed into his clothes and boots, while Adam told him the name of the lone man who had appeared for work. This man, Huggins, had no idea where the others were, Lloyd said, and he thought Huggins was telling the truth.

Moffat moved over to the washstand, doused cold water on his face, and combed his hair. A fight, he wondered? Or maybe a souse undertaken on the prospect of the good wages that were to be collected? Neither would account for the absence of all but one man on the shift, however.

He gave Adam orders to keep steam up until he returned, and then tramped over to the stables. Saddling his bay, he mounted and took the road down to Vermilion.

The sun had not yet touched anything but the Vermilion's highest peaks, and the frost lay white on the black pines, graying them. At Bone Creek, he jumped a doe with two fawns and listened to their almost noiseless flight into the timber.

The question of his shift, however, kept nagging persistently in his mind. Those eleven men could mine and move about twenty tons of ore a shift, and twenty tons of Dutch Surrency's ore was worth more than fifty thousand dollars, in silver, according to the assay. It was his obligation to see that the four shifts were kept working the clock around, he knew, or he wasn't worth his pay.

The town was awake and beginning work when he rode in, and he speculated on where to begin his search. Running over the names of the missing men, he found he did not know where any of them lived. A pair of them, Shaw and Card, had quit assessment work on their own claim to work for Dutch's wages, he remembered, but their prospect lay far up Bone Creek.

Reining in at the Comfort, he dismounted and considered. If there had been any wholesale trouble last night, the most likely place to find out about it would be in the saloons. Accordingly, he tramped down the steps of the Comfort and went inside.

The saloon was deserted except for a pair of freighters who were having a quick drink before they started work. The bartender, whom Moffat did not know, had just come on. No, there had been no fight and no carouse here last night. It would be easy enough to tell if there had been, he concluded dryly.

63

Outside the Comfort, Moffat halted and considered the town, baffled. He was wasting time, and every hour he spent here meant less ore moved from the Big Jay. Then he thought of Beaufort's Bunkhouse, and moved up the street toward it. It was a miner's place, and somebody there would know where his shift had disappeared.

He was at the corner of Timmy Malone's Silverbell saloon when a man came out the swing doors and nodded to him. Moffat slowed his pace, and abruptly changed course for the Silverbell. This was the miners' hangout, after work, and they might be able to tell him something in here.

The Silverbell was larger than the Comfort, and gaudier. The long bar was on the left, the gambling tables, with chairs stacked atop them at this early hour, on the right. At the rear was a dance floor, with the piano in the corner. It was too early for the girls to be at work, but the scent of their cheap perfume lingered like a stain in the big room.

A trio of idle millhands was gossiping with Timmy Malone, the swart, sour little man who owned the Silverbell. They were halfway down the long bar. The second bartender was stacking clean glasses on the backbar, and Moffat approached him.

"I'm from the Big Jay," Moffat began. "Seen anyone on our six o'clock shift?"

The bartender was a young man, and he gave Moffat a friendly but cynical grin. "No, sir, and I bet you didn't either."

"That's why I asked. Did they walk off?"

"They was bought off."

The bartender draped the towel over his shoulder and laid both hands on the bar. "Bill Taff come in last night and spread the word. Any Big Jay miners that want seven dollars a day for a six-hour shift can start work at the Ginger Queen, this noon. He'll top any Big Jay wage, Taff said."

Moffat was silent and the bartender came erect. "Prices are goin' up, ain't they, Bud?"

"That's right," Moffat said mildly. He thanked him, and when he reached the street he was smiling to himself. Halting in the road to let a team drag a load of timbers past him, he moved directly on up the hill and turned in Jarboe's office.

Jarboe, Bill Taff, and Max Howe were studying a plat of mine locations on the back wall. Only Max turned at his entrance, and then Jarboe, seeing Moffat, called in an amiable voice, "Hello, young fella. Come to sign on for seven dollars a day?"

"Not quite yet," Moffat said. He coolly appraised Taff, noting the condition of Taff's face, and then, ignoring Max, he settled his glance on Jarboe.

The old man sauntered over to his swivel chair and sat down, saying pleasantly, "Hear you're working for Dutch."

"Jarboe," Moffat said gently, "you better send one of your poodles around to the saloons and call off that seven-dollar-a-day wage. He better make it before the noon shift, too."

Jarboe's white eyebrows raised in mock surprise, but his tone was mild and gibing when he spoke. "Dutch can't afford it, eh?"

"Neither can you."

Jarboe smiled. "I can top any wages Dutch can pay. You won't have a miner working for you."

"You'll have a chance to, then," Moffat said. "Because by noon today, Dutch will start paying seventy dollars a day. Or would you rather make it a hundred and forty dollars a day? Or two hundred? Suit yourself."

There was a long thin silence in which Jarboe regarded him carefully, a puzzlement in his eyes. "That's bluff," he said then. "Dutch hasn't got the money."

"He's got it in the ground, Jarboe," Moffat gibed gently. "He's got a million dollars in the ground. If he has to, Dutch'll pay out every dollar of it in wages. He'll give away the ore free for the hauling before he'll leave it for you." He paused now, isolating this. "If you try to top his wages, Jarboe, you'll have to put out a million dollars. And you won't get the ore. Now do you want to gamble a million you will?"

Jarboe didn't answer, and now Moffat said gently, "Don't try buying our miners away from us, Jarboe. Noon's your deadline to renege on that seven-dollar wage. If you don't, you'd better start spending."

Moffat turned then and went out.

Jarboe steepled his fingers now and looked inquiringly at Bill Taff. Max Howe whistled softly in exclamation, but neither man paid him any attention.

Taff said wryly, "That's open and shut. What do you say, R. B.?"

"What do *you* say?" Jarboe asked thinly. "It was your idea."

Taff rubbed the back of his neck in a gesture of sheepishness. "I think they're Indian enough to do it."

Jarboe said with a wicked gentleness, "Now how are you feelin'? Can you get your hand in a trigger guard? Does he still look too big for you?"

Taff sat down resignedly. "All right. What do you want me to do?"

4

MOFFAT shoved his breakfast plate aside, leaned back in his chair, and packed his pipe, watching Candace move about the kitchen. Dutch, shirtless and with his galluses hanging in the rear, was again at the business Moffat's story had interrupted. He had a shard of mirror propped on the drainboard of the sink, and, scissors in hand, was trimming his beard, leaning over so that the clippings fell precisely on the paper he had spread for the purpose.

Finished, Dutch folded the paper, went over to the stove, lifted the lid, and carefully tilted the paper so the clippings fell in the fire. Folding the paper now, he glanced over at Moffat. "If that timbering crew is back for their wages, maybe I could put them at the head."

From the bedroom Spence Fuller's voice called, "Wouldn't be worth it, Dutch. They can't mine. Wait and see if the noon shift shows up."

Candace moved over to the stove from the sink. She said slyly, "Does it hurt that much to lose a little money, Dad?"

Dutch looked at her and growled, "Hell, no. It hurts to leave any ore for Jarboe."

Moffat and Candace exchanged glances, and Candace smiled. Dutch moved over to his shirt on the back of the chair, and Moffat lighted his pipe, rose, and carried his plate to the stack on the table by the sink.

Dutch said, "Larkin, you cruise the saloons this morning and see if you can pick up the noon shift. I'll go on up."

Moffat said he would, and halted by the curtained window where the sun, over the Bone Peaks, laid its bright morning light on the shedding alders. He heard Dutch go out, heard Candace moving behind him, and still he stared abstractedly out the window. They were wasting six hours of the precious eight days left them, and the thought galled him. There was no use rounding up the shift that had just gone off work; it would be noon before they could be at work again. He turned away from the window and restlessly prowled the kitchen, until he was hauled up by Candace.

"Don't be such a fire horse, Larkin. There's nothing you can do about it."

"But we aren't moving ore," Moffat growled.

Candace lifted the kettle from the stove and filled the dishpan at the sink. Returning the kettle, she said calmly, "We're a few tons less rich. I don't think we'll miss it."

Moffat, watching her, asked with a sudden curiosity, "What'll you do, once you're rich, Candace?"

Candace was in the act of putting the kettle back on the stove. Her movement was suddenly arrested, and she looked pensively at the kettle and set it down gently. The way her free hand slowly stroked her apron, the tilt of her head, the curve of her neck was a nice thing to watch, Moffat thought, and then she looked up at him. There was a shyness and a wistfulness in her dark eyes then that surprised him, and then it faded, giving way to a mocking humor. "Buy myself some hens." She turned back to the sink.

Moffat was immediately aware that his question, asked half in teasing, had touched some deep and private yearning in this girl. He supposed she had been poor enough always, with the smothered hungers of a girl who had lived in one rough frontier camp after another, and he had asked for her dreams. His question seemed an invasion of her privacy and an impertinence; and he

67

moved toward the door, angry with himself, saying, "You can't even buy the eggs unless we get the ore out."

He stepped outside, closing the door behind him, and knocked out his pipe, feeling an obscure guilt. He had overreached himself. Candace was only the daughter of the man he worked for, a girl who had met him at an ugly moment in his life, and to whom he had showed only obstinacy and cowardice and temper. His life would touch hers for only eight days longer, and she owed him nothing but civility.

Moving to the corner of the house he saw the wood-pile, and remembering Candace's words of the first night, he pocketed his pipe and tramped over to it.

He sawed up a length of jackpine with the bucksaw and was splitting it, feeling the sweet pleasure of handling dry timber with a sharp axe when he heard a movement behind him and turned. Candace, with the chip box beside her, was picking up chips. The sharp air had brought a color to her cheeks; as she knelt on the dry bed of chips, gathering them, she said cheerfully, "Now I know you've traveled, Larkin. I even know how you've traveled."

Moffat said cautiously, "Now, do you?"

"Only tramps chop wood for their breakfast."

Moffat laughed then, and Candace did too, and Moffat put his axe aside. Candace settled back on her heels, looking about at the fine morning, and Moffat sat himself on the chopping block. He wondered if she had sensed his embarrassment, and was trying to ease it by this visit. No, there was little artfulness in her, he thought, and as he watched her a simple pleasure in her company came to him.

She was looking above him at the distant Bone Peaks, and then her glance returned to him. "The elk will be coming down soon. This is a day to hunt." She smiled with a kind of self-derision. "I'm thinking of my Christmas mincemeat. It's no good without elk."

"Venison, yes. Elk, no."

"Elk makes the best," Candace said firmly. "Why doesn't it?"

"Because I lived a whole winter on elk meat once." His grimace brought a laugh from Candace.

"When was this?"

68

"Five years ago, when Charlie Storrs and I were making a prospect for Corona in Idaho."

Candace made a grimace now. "I'd have eaten Charlie Storrs."

Moffat laughed then. There was a kind of antic humor in Candace that was irresistible.

She smiled, almost guiltily, and said, "Well, he's smug, and smug people are always cruel." She was suddenly serious. "I was proud of you last night when you wouldn't let him bait you. He wanted to ride you, and when you didn't get mad, he lost his advantage."

"Something he seldom likes to lose," Moffat murmured.

"It must be contagious. His wife doesn't like to lose it, either." Her voice was tart.

Moffat grinned faintly. "Things weren't right between you when Charlie and I came back, last night. What happened?"

"Talk," Candace said curtly, and looked away.

"About me?"

She looked back at him swiftly. "You're being vain."

"I just know Josephine."

"Yes, very well, I'd say," Candace said dryly. She flushed then at the sharpness of her words, and again began to gather chips.

Moffat said gently, "So she told you we were to be married?"

Candace didn't glance up. "Why, yes, I think she mentioned it."

"Should I be ashamed of that?"

Candace looked up now and held his glance. "No. She's pretty enough. Maybe nice, too. I don't know."

Moffat, watching her, thought, *Tell her the rest.* And then he thought, *You've never figured it out for yourself. Why expect her to?*

Candace said suddenly, "Well, you look ashamed now."

Moffat nodded, and said quietly, "I ran out before the marriage, Candace."

Candace started to say something, and then didn't. She only watched him curiously.

"I'd had the bribe money from Pacific Shares for a week."

Candace asked shrewdly, "Why did you take it?"

"For her," Moffat said slowly. "I wanted to give her

everything she'd never had. She was hungry for it, like a man gets hungry for meat, and she'd never had anything."

Candace kept silent, and Moffat was silent too, reaching for words with which to frame this memory. "But once I had the bribe money, it spoiled it. I knew if I'd done this because of her, I'd do anything because of her. I gave it away." He was watching Candace. "Do you understand that?"

Candace looked at him searchingly. "Yes, I guess I do, anyway."

Moffat's voice was grim now. "It wouldn't have worked. I would have stolen for her, lied for her, killed for her, even. And I think she would have let me. It couldn't work, and I knew it."

"So you ran?"

"So I ran."

A faint, wise smile touched Candace's face. "Are you ashamed of being honorable?"

"Was it honorable to run?"

"No. But it would have been more dishonorable to stay." She looked down at her box of chips and said softly, "You're your own man now, Larkin." She looked up. "Aren't you? Could it happen to you again if she weren't Mrs. Storrs?"

"No."

"Then it turned out right."

Candace began to pick up chips aagin, and Moffat watched her, not really seeing her, but turning over in his mind what she had said. He was aware, without it meaning anything to him, that Candace kept looking at him, and he picked up a chip and slowly broke it to pieces, thinking of what she had said.

Her voice cut in on his thoughts, "Why don't you say it, Larkin?"

He looked up at her, puzzled. "Say what?"

"That there ought to be a nice hardwood gag made for meddling women like me."

He came to his feet, and she picked up her box of chips and rose too. Her face wore a deep flush, and she watched him with a kind of fierce embarrassment. He said, "I didn't even think it. Why should I?"

"I led you on."

70

Moffat frowned. "Led me on where?"

"I——" She hesitated, and then said in dismal embarrassment, "Oh, hell," and turned and ran toward the corner of the house.

When she had vanished, Moffat stood motionless a full minute, casting back over the conversation. He could make nothing of her words, and even less of her embarrassment.

Presently, he turned to the chopping block again and resumed work, and he lost the morning in hard unthinking labor.

Afterward, when a look at the sun told him it was past midmorning, he loaded his arms with wood and tramped back to the house. Candace was busy at the stove and would not look at him. Moffat stacked his wood and moved over to his coat and put it on, then took his hat from the wall.

He tramped over to the doorway of Spence's room and said, "Anything I can send you by Dutch?"

"A new set of ribs," Spence growled, and then he raised his head and said, "Yes, by thunder! A razor. Dutch shaves with scissors."

Moffat waved good-bye to him and wheeled and said, passing the table, "That was a good breakfast, Candace."

She was stirring something at the stove, and now she stopped, but Moffat had reached the door before she looked over her shoulder. She said then, "Women are crazy, Larkin; I never knew how crazy until today. Now go on. Good-bye."

Moffat stepped out, a beginning smile on his face. This was a strange girl, with a bright quicksilver way of talking about her, and he didn't pretend to understand her thoughts. He only knew that he liked to be with her, and that even the telling of how he had known Josephine had been easy, without the old feeling of shame.

He caught his horse, which had been grazing in the brush, tightened the cinch, slipped the bridle on, and mounted, putting him on the footpath among the alders.

By the time he reached the road, his mind was again on the noon shift. Tying his horse at the Comfort's tie rail, he watched the late-morning traffic for a moment, wondering if Jarboe had reneged on his wage offer by now. He would be lucky if he could raise half his shift, he thought. Because it was custom for most of the miners to stroll up from Beaufort's bunkhouse to pick up a drink at Timmy Malone's Silverbell before going to work, he turned toward that saloon for the beginning of his search.

Approaching the swing doors, he heard an overtone of loud talk and laughter, and he shoved through the door. The two big overhead lamps were lighted against the dimness of the interior, but it was a murky, smoke-roiled light, and Moffat halted just inside the door to let his eyes adjust themselves to the gloom.

The chairs were off the tables now, placed around the gambling tables. At one table, two dealers and three burly floormen were playing an uneasy game of poker while they watched the crowd.

The bar was jammed with miners and millhands, and Moffat saw one of his noon shift, a stubby miner named Manahan, bellied up to the bar at its near end.

He moved in beside Manahan, and promptly saw the man was drunk. Glancing down the bar, he saw another pair of Big Jay miners, both on the noon shift, and they were both flushed with liquor. His curiosity sharpened as he looked them over.

Timmy Malone, whiskey bottle in hand, cruised back up the bar, pouring occasional drinks. He was a dark, cheerless man, small and feisty of manner, and he stopped in front of Manahan. "You're Big Jay, ain't you?"

Manahan nodded, and without another word, Malone filled his glass.

Moffat said, "So am I, Timmy. What does it buy me?"

Malone glanced at him and said lazily. "Hello, Moffat. It buys you free drinks."

"Who's paying?"

Malone said indolently, "Bill Taff. He had to back water on that seven-dollar wage. He bought a barrel of booze from me and said to pass it out to the Big Jay crew and tell 'em to forget it."

A slow wrath stirred in Moffat then. Jarboe was beaten on the wage raise, but he had contrived to get the noon shift too drunk to work. He'd got what he wanted, a further delay of work at the Big Jay.

72

Moffat said reasonably, "But that's my noon shift you're getting soused."

Malone shrugged. "Fire 'em, then."

"You better cork the bottle, Timmy," Moffat said, still quietly.

Malone looked at him belligerently. "You run your mine, and I'll run my bar."

Moffat nodded equably, and Malone turned away. Moffat came erect, took a deep breath of resignation, and cuffed Manahan lightly on the arm. "Working today, my friend?"

Manahan, who had been listening with a drunken dignity, tried to focus his eyes on Moffat. He failed, but he said stoutly, "I am looking to fight first."

Realizing the hopelessness of trying to move out this drunk and probably belligerent crew, Moffat pushed away from the bar, went out, turned the corner, and cut angling across the road to Paxton's livery stable. Skirting the leaking water trough with its fringe of viscous red mud, he entered the small log office and found a hostler mending harness. He asked, "Ed, what can I rent that'll hold ten men?"

Ed thought a moment. "Mudwagon?"

"I want high sides. A driver too. They're drunk."

"An ore wagon, then."

"Hook it up," Moffat said.

He stepped out and looked across at the Silverbell. There was the guarantee of a riot implicit in what he was planning but he was going through with it, anyhow. He considered the number and the make-up of the Big Jay miners he had seen in the Silverbell, and he thought it unlikely there was a gun among them.

Accordingly, he tramped down the street past the hotel and two doors beyond it he climbed the stairs of a store which bore the sign, Hardware and Miners' Supplies. He purchased a half-dozen hickory pickhandles and returned to the Silverbell, this time to the back door. At the corner of the building, he threw the pickhandles in the high weeds by the back door and pushed inside.

There were a half-dozen noisy arguments in progress at the bar, and it seemed to Moffat that the talk had

73

risen in pitch since he'd left. But so far there were no open fights, thanks to the four heavy-shouldered floormen who were cruising the crowd now.

Moffat waited until he caught the eye of one of the floormen, and then he beckoned to him. The man was a truculent-seeming giant, with black hair that grew down on his forehead almost to the bridge of his nose. A look of suspicion was in his heavy face as he approached, and Moffat wondered if Malone had warned his men to be on the lookout for the Big Jay management.

Moffat said, "Look, friend. I want to talk to Andy Freed, my hoist man." He identified a towering black-haired man in the middle of the bar. The floorman looked back at him, and his suspicion had deepened. Moffat said, "No, I don't want any fuss or any trouble. Just move him out back. Whatever you do, don't break up the fun."

"You don't want trouble?" the floorman asked in bafflement.

Moffat said innocently, "Why would I? Let them alone." And when the floorman didn't answer, Moffat held out a gold eagle and said, "Buy yourself a cigar."

The floorman accepted it, thanked him, still with suspicion, and Moffat stepped out the back door. He put his back to the wall and waited, watching the ore wagon being harnessed in the road in front of Paxton's.

Presently the door opened and big Andy Freed came out. He took one step out the door, looked about him, saw Moffat, came to a halt and faced him. He swayed a little on his feet, and his face was flushed, and he would have loved nothing better than a fight, Moffat knew.

Moffat just looked at him. Andy said then in a voice thick with whiskey, "You want me?"

"No," Moffat said.

"That feller said you did."

Moffat smiled faintly, "Looks like Timmy Malone is moving you boys out, doesn't it?"

Andy stared at him in frowning concentration, still weaving in a slow teeter. He said, "Hunh?"

"Malone's pushing you out, it looks like. The whiskey you boys are drinking is already paid for. If he kicks you Big Jay boys out, he'll be able to sell the rest of the whiskey."

74

Andy thought that over with an alcoholic carefulness, and then turned abruptly, headed for the door.

"Wait a minute," Moffat said. He stooped down and got a pickhandle and extended it to Andy. "Those floor-men use sawed-off pool cues."

Andy accepted the pickhandle and hefted it. Moffat said, "I've got some more. You better get some help, though."

Andy grinned and went back in the saloon. It was not more than ten seconds before the din exploded to a roar. Presently, a pair of miners boiled through the back door at the same time, and one of them stumbled and fell on his face. Moffat had the pickhandles waiting. They accepted them without even looking at him and ran back into the saloon. There was a howling racket inside now, and Moffat saw the two hostlers across the street pause in their harnessing and look toward the saloon. A shotgun boomed inside, and Moffat smiled grimly. That would be Malone letting off at the ceiling in the futile hope of quelling the riot his whiskey had fired.

Within the next few minutes, all his pickhandles had been distributed to Big Jay miners who were drunk to a man, all eager for a fight.

When the last pickhandle was gone, he crossed over to the ore wagon and said to Ed, who was harnessing, "Drive it around in front of the Silverbell when you're done, Ed."

"What's goin' on in there?" Ed asked.

"Just a friendly fight."

Now Moffat headed back across the street, listening to the full swell of the riot inside. By instigating the fight, which would have been inevitable anyway, he had cemented the Big Jay into one aggrieved and loyal unit. Now it was up to him to get them out before too many heads were cracked.

Stepping inside the rear door, he looked at the scene. It was a boiling riot in here, and he could see the pale pickhandles slashing down in the murky dimness of the room. A pair of miners were slugging it out with the young bartender on the bartop, while Timmy Malone hacked at their feet with a whiskey bottle. Tables and chairs were overturned, the piano long since dumped on its face. Every man in the room, it seemed to Moffat, had joined the mêlée, which had centered in the middle of the bar.

Moffat kept to the wall and moved into the room, watching. The Big Jay crew, in spite of the pickhandles, was getting the worst of it, as he had known they would. The free whiskey they had consumed, besides making them slow and befuddled, had earned them the envy of every other millhand and miner in the room, and they were being ganged.

Moffat circled until he was near the front of the room, and then he hefted a chair. Reaching out for the shoulder of the closest man, he spun him around and out of the fight, and then picking up the chair and holding it before him, he rammed into the mêlée, legs driving.

His charge bowled over a pair of miners in front of him, driving them to their knees and breaking a hole for him to the core of the fight. Ahead of him and to the right he saw the four floormen ranked in a loose line, centering their attack on Andy and another Big Jay miner. All six of them were hacking wildly, aimlessly, ferociously, pool cues against pickhandles. Moffat raised his chair and stepped in beside Andy and swung the chair in a low half-circle that caught a pair of miners waist-high. One of them yelled and backed off, and again Moffat swung the chair, and this time he was given clearance.

He stepped in now, lifting his chair, and brought it angling down on the nearest floorman. He heard the rungs break on the man's head and then the heavy seat smashed down on him, beating the man to his knees. The companion floorman saw it and backed off, and now Moffat turned to Andy.

"Back up!" he shouted. "Get out the front!"

His last words were choked off as a solid weight straddled his back. He would have fallen to his knees if he had not staggered onto his chair. He felt the man on his back try to clamp knees on his back and fail, and then skid off. Across the chair, Moffat saw a kick coming and he turned and took it on his shoulder before he straightened up, free of his burden. He swiped viciously at the kicker, and missed him.

Andy had heard him, and was falling back with his companion through the narrow alley formed by the bar

76

and the Big Jay crew being slowly backed against it. Moffat stepped back into this alley too, and Malone's men, sensing victory, charged, their pool cues swinging.

It was a wild mêlée then. Moffat took a stunning blow on his upper arm that paralyzed it for a moment. He had no notion of the direction in which it came, or if he had been hit accidentally by one of his own crew. He swung his shattered chair with savage abandon, dodging and parrying blows from a pair of pickhandles in the hands of miners who had wrested them from Big Jay men. And all the time he was backing steadily, Andy beside him.

The floormen made their last concerted rush when the Big Jay crew was almost out the door. Backing, Moffat tripped and went down, caroming into bodies as he fell. Andy stepped into the breach he left and Moffat scrambled to his feet. With a looping overhand movement he threw the chair past Andy's shoulder into the floormen, reached down and caught the collar of the downed man and dragged him past the swing doors and down the steps.

Andy came backing out, paused long enough to throw his pickhandle, and then he leaped out onto the cinder path.

Moffat had a brief look about him. The millwagon was pulled up some ten feet away, and between it and the Silverbell were a half-dozen bloody Big Jay hands. Some were standing, leaning on their pickhandles; others were sitting down, holding bloody heads, and more than one lay flat in the dirt where he had fallen or been dragged. Moffat's glance swiveled to the Silverbell. In the doorway framed by broken sagging swing doors, the big floorman stood. He had a pool cue in one hand and a pickhandle in the other and he raised a bloody arm and pointed with the pickhandle at Andy.

"Now I'll learn you something," he said flatly, and he stepped out of the doorway, a second floorman behind him.

Moffat reached for his gun, moving it at the same time, and when his gun was out he halted in front of the floorman and they met solidly.

"Back off!" Moffat said. "The fun's over."

The floorman started to raise his pickhandle when he saw Moffat's gun. His motion was arrested, and slowly then, he let the pickhandle settle to his side. He looked over the Big Jay crew with eyes still hot with anger, and then he turned and entered the saloon. Somewhere inside, a scuffle was still going on.

Moffat holstered his gun then, and turned to look over his crew. They were a sorry lot, bloody and not quite sober, and oddly cheerful, even if subdued. The more sober of them eyed him contritely, wondering what was coming. The drunker of them, among them Manahan, who was leaning against the big rear wheel of the mill-wagon, a bloody pickhandle still clenched in his hand, were still talkative. Manahan was saying, "Man, 'twas like the fair at Donnybrook when I was a lad."

Hardly anybody laughed; the talk was tapering off, and they were regarding Moffat now. What had started out as their refusal to work for him had turned into a brawl from which he had rescued them. Moreover, it was plain enough he had fought with them. It was occurring to them that they were probably out of a job, after such a show.

Moffat let them wait a moment, while he counted them. When he had reached six, one more of his crew who had been pitched out the back door came around the corner to join the group. Altogether, there were nine here. Moffat looked them over and grunted, and began to move, saying, "Well, if five dollars a day still looks good, climb in the wagon and report to Dutch."

He tramped past them then, heading for Paxton's watering trough and a wash. His noon shift, he knew, would move ore today.

Josephine was seated on the bed, the mirror propped on the chair before her, brushing her hair when Charlie came up from his early dinner and entered the room. Josephine tilted back her head, shook out her dark hair, and sighed, folding her hands in her lap.

"What is it about this place? I get tired even brushing my hair."

"You're a couple of miles up, almost," Charlie grunted. He moved over to his valise and started rummaging around in it.

"Boiled potatoes again for dinner?" Josephine asked.

"And good ones, too," Charlie said.

"There's no such thing as a good boiled potato," Josephine replied. She looked at herself in the mirror as she said, "I'll be as big as Mrs. Barber before I get out of here. Where are you going this afternoon?"

"I've got to look over some property by the Big Jay. Want to go?"

"No."

"What'll you do?"

"Work up some hysterics, I suppose," Josephine said. She yawned. "I can use up an hour in the dining room, pushing those boiled potatoes around on my plate. Then I can go look over the mops, pans, and axes in both stores, then I can take a walk till I'm out of breath, then I can sit in the lobby an hour, then I can——"

"You lead a hell of a life," Charlie said amiably. "Go meet some women." He found the box of cigars he was looking for, laid it on the washstand and began to fill his cigar case from it. He looked as cheerful and vital and busy as always, Josephine thought with a mixture of envy and wonder.

"Mrs. Barber?" Josephine asked dryly. "I get tired of being insulted to my face."

"There's that Surrency girl," Charlie suggested.

Josephine glanced at him sharply, exasperation in her expression. "Honestly, Charlie, you're impossible."

Charlie looked up, wonder in his eyes, and Josephine said, "She's out to catch Larkin. I told you."

"Does that take her voice away?" Charlie asked. "I thought you wanted company."

"Not that kind."

Charlie snorted. "My God, anybody'd think you were protecting your only son from a fortune hunter. Why worry who gets that crook?"

Josephine gave him a wicked glance which he did not see. He pocketed his cigar case, returned the box to his valise and came over to the bed. As he leaned down to kiss her, Josephine turned her cheek.

Charlie said, "I'm not your cousin, dear," and reached out and turned her head to him and kissed her full on the mouth. She submitted unenthusiastically, and then resumed brushing her hair as Charlie tramped over to the door.

He paused then, said dryly, "Try piccalilli on those potatoes. It helps," and opened the door and went out.

Josephine yawned and resumed brushing her hair. Charlie's heavy-handed humor, seldom entertaining, seemed even less so this morning. As she put up her hair, she thought with a bleak distaste of the long afternoon stretching before her. But it was not the same distaste she had felt yesterday; last night, seeing the Surrency girl and Larkin together had changed that. Now, she felt a morbid and depressing curiosity about the two of them, and had no idea how to satisfy it.

Rising now, she returned the mirror to its place on the washstand and then halted at the window to look out onto the busy noontime street. She saw two men standing in front of the saloon across the street. One of them spoke to his companion and pointed up to her window. Suddenly aware she was in her camisole, she backed out of sight, an anger and disgust in her. This was typical of this whole dirty, rough and disgusting camp. *Then go home. What's keeping you here?* she asked herself. She knew what it was, and for the first time she put it into words, *She's out to get him and I don't like it.* Once the words were framed, she considered them with the close practicality of her sex, admitting their truth and wondering what she should do about it.

She slipped on her shirtwaist and suit coat, made a final adjustment to her hair, and left the room. Halfway down the stair, she saw the usual noontime groups of men milling in the lobby.

Passing the desk, she saw Mrs. Barber and said coldly, "Good morning."

"It's noon," Mrs. Barber said loudly. "Have a good sleep?"

"Not on that bed, my dear," Josephine said sweetly, and moved on toward the dining room.

She was almost to the doorway when Larkin Moffat came out, heading for the outside door.

"Larkin!" Josephine called.

Moffat hauled up and looked about him and saw her approaching. He was, Josephine thought with a faint stirring of excitement, pleased to meet her. He smiled his slow smile and when she came to halt in front of him, he said, "Better hurry if you want a place."

80

"Oh, I've eaten long since," Josephine lied. "I was going out on an errand. Come along."

She put a hand on his arm and they went out and down the steps to the plankwalk, where Moffat paused. "Which way?"

Josephine looked up at him and said gravely, "I lied to you, Larkin. I'm not going on an errand. I'm just bored crazy."

Moffat regarded her with a humorous sympathy. "Well, it isn't exactly San Francisco."

"Where are you going? Can I go with you?" Josephine asked impetuously. She flushed a little then under his steady quizzical gaze, and then said, "Charlie's gone off and left me. I haven't seen you, anyway. Can I tag along wherever you're going and we can talk?"

Moffat nodded. "I was going up to my shack to clean it up and pick up a few things."

Josephine squeezed his arm. "I'll be good, and I'll help." She was aware then of a trio of men approaching. Quickly she took her hand from Moffat's arm, as the smaller man in dark business clothes doffed his hat to her. The second man, older and in rough clothes did likewise. Bill Taff was the third man. He touched the brim of his hat.

"Hello, Mr. Bishop, Mr. Hazeltine, Mr. Taff."

"Afternoon, Mrs. Storrs," the three of the men said. They smiled politely to her, and then their glances shifted to Moffat. Bishop, the closest and tidiest of the trio, looked stonily past Moffat. Hazeltine turned his glance aside to the steps, ignoring him. Taff nodded gravely, mockingly.

Josephine, quickly sensing the snub, waited until they had gone up the steps, then asked in a teasing voice, "What have you done to them, Larkin?"

"Kept out of jail," Larkin said dryly. "Shall we go?"

Josephine felt the color mount in her face, and with it came an angry resentment at these new friends of Charlie's. She had forgotten, clumsily, as she teased Larkin, that his reputation here in Vermilion was now destroyed, and that Charlie had been responsible for this. For a moment, walking down the road alongside Larkin, she hated Charlie for what he had done.

She walked silently, almost meekly, beside Moffat, occasionally giving him an oblique glance, trying to read his thoughts. He was a friendless man now, she supposed, but strangely enough, he had none of the solitary man's stiffnecked pride about him. Had the friendship of the Surrencys made up for everything else he had lost, she wondered? The thought was not comforting.

Josephine had difficulty walking in the dry ruts of the red road, and when they turned off it to climb the hill, she was thankful.

They stopped in front of the shack then to catch their breath. Josephine noticed the boarded window now, and asked in bewilderment, "Aren't you living here now? Why is it boarded up?"

"I'm living at the mine. Candace had some kids board it up after Taff wrecked it."

"After she snooped, I suppose," Josephine said tartly.

"She didn't mention that," Moffat replied calmly.

Josephine's lip lifted derisively, but Larkin was not even looking at her. He was undoing the wire that held the door to its hasp, and now he pushed the door open and stepped inside. Josephine followed him in and stopped beside him, looking over the monumental disorder of the room. The complete and wanton wreckage appalled her, and she said wrathfully, "Charlie should be ashamed of this."

"Maybe he is," Larkin said mildly, and moved into the room. Glass and cinders crunched under his feet as he moved over to the packing case which had held his furnace coke. The contents had been spilled, and he picked up the box, wiped it clean with a wad of paper lying on the floor, and set it beside the desk, saying, "My only chair seems to be broken."

Josephine sat down and watched him prowl around the room. First he looked in the room beyond and then wheeled and came back to the big bench, where, hands on hips, he stood looking at the wreckage. To Josephine, this was the first real moment of intimacy they had had, and she examined him critically and carefully, comparing him with the man she had known. He was thinner, and therefore seemed taller, and there was both a hardness and a patience about him, even in his lean face, that was new and strange. But it was his self-sufficiency that was so alien. She remembered the quiet adoration with which he used to watch her, the hunger for her presence and her beauty that she used to read so easily in his eyes. It wasn't there now. She wanted suddenly to make him recall those times, but she was wise enough to know she must proceed with caution.

She said, "I never knew you could assay, Larkin."

"Corona taught me that," he said absently.

"It's lucky they did, or you wouldn't have a job now."

Larkin kept studying the disorder of the bench, and seemed to have only half heard what she said. A couple of seconds later he glanced up at her. "Why is that?"

"Didn't you do Surrency's assay?"

"Oh, that, yes." He turned away from the bench and came over and regarded the wrecked furnace.

"What kind of people are they, Larkin?" Josephine asked slyly.

Frowning, still looking at the furnace, Moffat said, "Surrencys? The best. He started as a leaser on a block over in a Leadville mine. He's still carrying some Confederate grapeshot in his side, and he couldn't stick the work. But he made a good prospect over West, sold out for a small stake, and started leasing big stuff."

"How old is she?"

"Candace? Oh, twenty-some."

"Just a baby," Josephine said, with a carelessness that covered the malice.

Moffat glanced at her, then, a faint humor stirring in his green eyes. "There are no baby women, just like there are no baby tigers."

"Oh, I noticed it, too," Josephine said quickly. "She's hard and catty."

Larkin's face altered into soberness. "You didn't understand, Josephine. I made a bad joke, I guess. Candace isn't hard and she isn't catty. She can just take care of herself."

Josephine felt the color coming into her face, felt a wicked anger stirring now. She'd walked into a simple trap, only Larkin hadn't even been trying to trap her. But, rightly or wrongly, she had brashly committed herself, and she knew she couldn't back down.

"I didn't like her," she said levelly.

Moffat shrugged. "Your privilege," he said, and went back to his study of the assay furnace.

This was getting her nowhere, Josephine saw; Larkin didn't even care enough about her opinion to argue. The thought was suddenly unbearable, and she knew a moment of bleak uncertainty. *I had him once. He can't have forgotten,* she told herself bitterly, and she watched him kneel close to her and test the bricks of the furnace. The turn of his head, the small-boy intentness, the thick dark hair, the soiled bandage on his scarred and muscular hand, his very nearness to her suddenly filled her with an overwhelming sense of her loss. She thought then, with a fathomless misery that held no surprise at all for her, *I still love him. I always will!* and she said, before she realized she was speaking, "Larkin."

He turned his head to look up at her.

"Nothing," she said in a shaky voice. "I just wondered if you remembered I was here." Her hands were so tightly clasped in her lap that her arms ached.

Moffat said easily, "Now, who would forget that?"

A kind of recklessness was in Josephine now, and she said bitterly, "Charlie does. Often."

Moffat watched her a second, and Josephine saw a faint puzzlement mount into his green eyes. He said easily, "Charlie just concentrates hard."

"On everything but me," Josephine said. She was heedless now, watching him with close, almost unbearable attention. She saw the puzzlement in his eyes alter now into withdrawal, into a kind of shrinking, and she leaned forward, utterly without reserve or caution. "I made a mistake, Larkin. A terrible, terrible mistake! So did you!"

He came to his feet, and Josephine rose too, facing him. Larkin said gently, "Don't, Josephine."

"But we could have been so wonderful together! Nobody would ever have been like us!"

She saw the withdrawal still, saw him going farther and farther away from her, and she said desperately, "Why did you go?"

"I had to," Larkin said quietly. "I wasn't any kind of a man, Josephine. I was all yours. I would have killed for you." He paused, and then said, still quietly, almost wonderingly, "I think I would have killed myself, if you had asked me to."

For a stunned moment Josephine heard and accepted this, and then a fierce elation swelled within her. "Oh,

84

Larkin, don't you see? That doesn't change! That can't ever leave you! You can't let go of me!"

She came to him then, throwing her arms about him and pressing her cheek roughly to his chest. "Oh, Larkin, Larkin," she said softly. "Let's both go this time! Damn Charlie! Damn them all! We're meant for each other!"

Even as she spoke, even through the unbearable joy that was in her, she was aware that Larkin had not even raised his arms, that he was standing still as stone.

She clung to him a moment longer, waiting for his response, and when it did not come she backed slowly away from him and tilted her head up to see his face. It was patient, full of pity, sad.

She struck at him, then, her open palm clouting him across the face with a slap like a gunshot.

He did not move, nor did his expression change. Seeing this, all the hope died in her. There was not even fury left, only a shame and humiliation.

"It's that Surrency girl," she said bitterly. "You fool! You fool!"

She wheeled then, and ran blindly out the door and down the hill.

Presently, Moffat moved to the door and looked down the hill. Josephine was out of sight. He turned slowly and glanced back over the room, not really seeing it. He had, he knew, just seen something that was both sad and ugly, and he thought of it wonderingly. In these three years since he had last seen Josephine, she had married Charlie Storrs and lived her life with him, and yet she did not love Charlie and had never loved him. She had been wildly eager to throw away that life and Charlie, too, if she could live with him, and the irony of it did not escape him. Where once he had run from that insensate need for her, she now felt the same insensate need for him, and he pitied her with the pity of understanding.

Presently, he moved back into the room and began to sort out the undamaged gear in the wreckage. But his mind kept returning to Josephine, and to a cold and wry assessment of himself. If, three years ago, Josephine had said to him what she said this afternoon, would he have left her? He didn't know. He did know, however, that he had been truthful to Candace this morning.

Josephine had no power over him now; the old feeling toward her was burned out and dead.

He stacked the salvaged whole gear in a corner, where Dutch would pick it up later. With what was left him of his equipment, and with what remained of an assay outfit at the Big Jay, he could round up enough gear to run a continuing assay on Dutch's ore later in the week. He wired the door shut, went down the hill, and turned toward the Comfort.

Mounting, he pulled his horse around and glanced over at the hotel. Bill Taff stood with shoulder against the door frame, watching him and Moffat grinned derisively at him. Taff turned and went inside.

Turning downstreet, he took the valley road toward the Big Jay, and his mind was still full of what had passed at his shack. It came to him, then, that twice Josephine in her recklessness had slurred Candace, and had even assumed that because of Candace he did not love her still. That was the classic face of jealousy, he supposed, and he smiled, thinking how Candace would protest in rage at Josephine's words, also knowing he would never repeat them to her.

He passed an ore wagon from the Total Eclipse and waved to the teamster as he passed. The thick stand of pines along the road touched the air with a winelike resin scent; and the blown aspen leaves, still yellow, dappled the darkness under the pines and spread across the road.

Turning off at the Big Jay dug road he presently approached Bone Creek and dismounted among the alders and had a long drink. A whistlepig on the far bank scolded him and gave the alarm as he crossed the stream, and he heard the alarm passed on down the creek by others.

Later, rounding the last bend in the road before the Big Jay, he saw Dutch standing below the ore bin in conversation with a mucker. The silver torrent of ore was cascading down the finished chute now and spilling out on Dacy's claim, raising a hollow rumble in the afternoon that shut out the sounds of mine machinery.

Afterward, he stabled his horse and went down to the stope to check his crew. Only one trammer was missing, and the rest, bloody but no longer drunk, were being harried mercilessly by Adam. He drove them with curses and threats which normally would have led to blows, but the crew was too beaten to fight.

Moffat filled in for the missing trammer until time to set off charges, before shift changes, and afterwards shared Adam's supper with him. Dutch came down with the six o'clock shift for his nightly prowl before leaving, and afterward Moffat remained until half the shift was completed.

He realized, suddenly, that he was bone-weary. He went up top and made the rounds, hauling up at last on the lip of the ore in the chill night. They had lost one shift's work today, but the ore bin was empty and the chute functioning, and he was satisfied.

Turning toward the office, he entered, blew the wall lamp, and moved into his cubbyhole bedroom, where he set the lamp on the table and then sagged to his bunk, stupid with weariness.

He was bending over his boots, then, when the blast came. It was sharp, close, and he was on his feet before it had vanished, before the other sound started.

He could hear this sound even above the patter of small rock falling on the roof; it was the sound of rock sliding, a blood-chilling, ponderous grinding that shook every rafter and joist in the shack.

Moffat grabbed the lantern and lunged through the door. Outside, he saw by the lantern in the hoist shack that the hoistman had left his job. He was standing by the door of the hoist shack, peering north in the direction of the road where the thunderous clatter of sliding rock was only now diminishing.

Moffat called wrathfully, "Get back to your job!" and then wheeled and ran toward the ore bin. On its lip, he could see nothing, and he hung the bale of the lantern over his arm and climbed down the log butts of the ore bin. Even now, he could hear the crashing thunder of the loose boulders battering their juggernaut way down the slope below, starting other slides and crashing trees.

Below the ore bin, he smelled the first hot dust of the rock slide, and now he stumbled down the slope, following the course of the chute.

And then he hauled up abruptly, for the chute had come to an end. Lifting his lantern high above him, he looked out at the silver river of rock that had wiped out the chute and the trestle that carried it across the wash.

Now, without even cursing, he started uphill, following up the slide, and when he came to the place where the dug road should be, he saw that had been wiped out, too. Someone, Jarboe's man, of course, had set off a charge in the gully above the road, and the charge had channeled the slide into the gully, wiping out road and chute.

Slowly, then, he lowered his lantern, comprehending this at last. The chute was gone, and the road on which timber for a new chute must be hauled was gone, too. Jarboe had sealed off his ore.

5

BILL TAFF carefully folded the last of six fried eggs into a size that would go between his bruised lips and downed it, drank his coffee, and rising, reached for the toothpicks in the glass. Putting one toothpick in his mouth, another in his shirt pocket, he fumbled a coin out of his pocket and tossed it on the table. It rolled under the feet of a miner eating opposite him, but Taff ignored it and stepped outside. On the cinder path, he halted and moodily picked his teeth, glancing idly at the open door of Jarboe's office next the restaurant.

The old man would be at the mill now, he knew, and he threw away his toothpick and turned uphill. This, he knew, was a morning in his life he would remember, and he speculated on what it would bring. The time had come to make his gamble; his chances of winning, considering the news he was bringing, were good, and he reviewed them again. All in all, his cards, if played right, were all a man could ask for.

It was cloudy today, and cold, with streamers of mist obscuring both mountains and hanging just above the serrated roof of the mill. As he walked on, he became aware of something strange about the morning, and it took him a moment to realize just what it was. The mill wasn't working, the insistent pulsing of the stamps was stilled. That meant the mill had broken down. The old man would be mad, and the madder he was this morning, Taff reflected, the better chances of the scheme. He grinned in anticipation.

He shrugged his burly shoulders deeper into his duck jacket and tramped on, passing the mill's machine shop. The mill had been built into the steep slope of Bone Mountain in a series of three ascending steps; Taff climbed to the middle level and opened the door that let onto the battery of stamps.

Immediately, he saw the group of men collected around number one battery; there was Jarboe and Slater, the mill boss, a machinist, and a scattering of millhands.

As he approached he heard the machinist say plaintively, "It ain't that. Can't you understand, R. B., even iron'll wear out?"

"That stem was new in June," Jarboe said grimly.

"It was fifth-hand in June," the machinist corrected him.

Jarboe glanced up and saw Taff now, and he said in a quiet snarl, "Where have you been?"

Taff said indolently, "Eating," and looked at the battery. The stem on number nine stamp had pulled its guide and broken. When he glanced back at Jarboe, he saw the wicked temper in the old man's eyes, and he regarded him with an amused insolence.

Jarboe said to Slater now, "Don't stand there! Blacksmith it! Fix it!" He looked at Taff and said, "Come along."

Taff followed him down the steps to the next level, where the concentrating tables were ranked. Jarboe went through a door in the end wall, and Taff followed him into the mill office.

It was a small room, as mussed and untidy as Jarboe himself, and Taff closed the door and watched Jarboe tramp across the room to the barrel chair by the stove.

"Damn jokers," Jarboe growled. "The whole crew of 'em haven't enough brains to pack in the head of one honest mucker."

Taff unbuttoned his coat and came across the room, saying dryly, "Nobody can do a job with junk, R. B."

He toed the chair in front of Slater's desk so that it

faced out into the room and slacked into it, yawning.

"What took you so long?" R. B. asked sharply.

"I told you. I ate. Try spending a night at timberline and see if you get hungry."

"Well, what happened?" Jarboe said impatiently.

Taff yawned again and slowly crossed his legs, slowly raised his glance to Jarboe. "It slid, all right. Wiped out the chute and covered a long stretch of the road."

Jarboe's cross expression altered into one of pleasure; he smiled, and reached in his coat pocket and pulled out his plug of tobacco. He was rummaging around in his trouser pocket for his knife, the expression of satisfaction still on his face, when Taff said dryly, "That's half what I saw."

Jarboe looked sharply at him.

Taff said, "When I left, Dutch had already rounded up a timbering crew again."

"Won't do 'em any good," Jarboe said. "They can't get the timber up there."

"They got it all right. You know where?" He paused, plain malice in his eyes. "Your bunkhouse and cook-shack. They had the roof off and were taking down the walls when I left."

Jarboe quit reaching for his knife; his hand stayed in his pocket and he just stared at Taff. "For a new chute?"

"For a new chute. Moffat'll have it finished by night."

Jarboe had found his knife. He withdrew it and slowly opened a blade, and then, as if the effort exhausted him, he leaned back in his chair and stared across the room. The framed plan and elevation of the mill that hung on the far wall seemed to fascinate him. He stared at it a long moment, knife in one hand, tobacco in the other.

Taff's voice was sharp and gibing, "You're getting poorer every hour. Your brains are getting softer every hour, too, R. B."

Jarboe flicked a wicked glance at him, and then set about carefully slicing a cnew from the plug.

"All rignt," Jarboe said mildly. "How's your brain— firm, hard, cold? Put it to work.'

"I have."

Jarboe was carefully slicing his plug, and he did not look up. "What does it tell you?"

"Kill him."

90

FLINT
IF HE HAD TO DIE, AT LEAST IT WOULD BE ON HIS TERMS..

Get a taste of the *true* West, beginning with the tale of *FLINT* FREE for 15 Days

Hunted by a relentless hired gun in the lava fields of New Mexico, Flint *"settled down to a duel of wits that might last for weeks...Surprisingly, he found himself filled with zest for the coming trial...So began the strange duel that was to end in the death of one man, perhaps two."*

If gripping frontier adventures capture your imagination, welcome to The Louis L'Amour Collection! It's a handsome, hardcover series of thrilling sagas by the world's foremost Western authority and author.

Each novel in The Collection is a true-to-life portrait of the Old West, depicted with gritty realism and striking detail. Each is enduringly bound in rich, Sierra-brown leatherette, with padded covers and gold-embossed titles. And each may be examined and enjoyed for 15 days. FREE. You are never under any obligation; so mail the card at right today.

Now in handsome Heritage Editions

Each matching 6" x 9" volume in The Collection is bound in rich Sierra-brown leatherette, with padded covers and embossed gold title... creating an enduring family library of distinction.

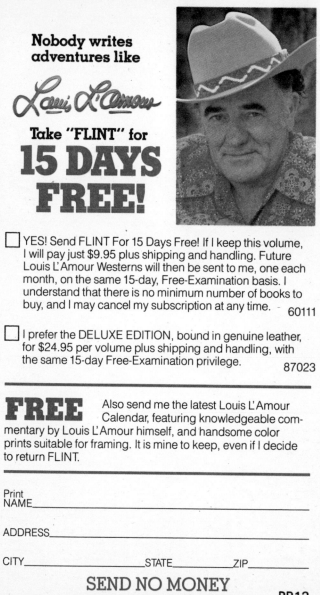

BUSINESS REPLY MAIL

FIRST CLASS   PERMIT NO. 2154   HICKSVILLE, N.Y.

Postage will be paid by addressee:

The

Louis L'Amour

Collection

Bantam Books
P.O. Box 956
Hicksville, New York 11802

Jarboe's head came up with a jerk. He looked long and levelly at Taff, who held his gaze steadily. It was Jarboe's glance that fell away first. He cut his chew, flipped it into his mouth, licked the blade on both sides, then pocketed knife and plug. Taff watched him closely, but the old man seemed carefully preoccupied with each small movement. Taff knew he was considering this, turning it over and over in his mind, shrinking from it, handling it with the caution it deserved.

Presently, Jarboe said mildly, "I don't like that."

"For a million dollars in silver, you could learn to like it," Taff said gently.

Jarboe said nothing; he pouched his tobacco in his cheek and essayed the first tentative chews, looking benignly at Taff. Then he said, "I'm an old man, Bill."

"A rich old man."

"I never owned a gun."

"A rich man that never owned a gun," Taff said.

"I wouldn't know how to go about it."

"A rich man that wouldn't know how to go about it." Jarboe frowned. "What are you trying to get at?"

"Just that you're rich."

"What's that got to do with it?"

Taff straightened his legs and smiled fleetingly. "You don't make your own clothes, do you? You don't mine your own ore, do you? You don't cook your own food, do you? You buy it done."

Jarboe said gently. "I see." He looked carefully at Taff. "A thousand dollars, Bill?"

Taff only sighed. He started to button up his coat with a deliberation that had something of finality in it.

"Bill, how much?" Jarboe said.

"You'd faint," Taff said idly.

"Wait a minute. How much?"

"You'd scream," Taff said.

"How much?" Jarboe repeated.

Taff finished buttoning his coat, looked coolly at him, and then said, "Half of what you get out of Dutch's strike when Moffat's dead."

Jarboe came out of his chair as if someone had booted him out of it. He gave Taff a venomous glance, and reached for his battered hat hanging on the wall, and put it on. Then he shrugged into his mackinaw, staring grimly at the floor. Taff watched him, an open amusement in his pale eyes.

Jarboe turned then and started briskly for the outside door. Nearly to it, his step began to lag and finally he stopped. He was doing some close thinking, Taff knew. Then he halted and turned. He had said tentatively, almost with abstraction, "If this happened, you'd have to trust me. I wouldn't sign anything."

"You'll pay me," Taff said, the meaning in his words plain enough."

"I wouldn't want to know anything about it."

"That's my worry."

"I don't hold with it, you understand."

"Hold with an accident? Nobody does." Taff grinned.

"It can't come back to me in any way."

"Not in any way you'd be legally responsible."

A look of anguish crossed the old man's face, and Taff wached him coldly and calculatingly, thinking with astonishment *Well, I've won. He's going to do it.*

"In fact," Jarboe said desperately, "I forbid you to do it. You've not got my consent in any way, shape or form."

Taff eyed him carefully, and then said, "Still, if he meets with an accident and Dutch had bad luck, that would naturally leave things open for me to be your partner in mining out Dutch's pocket."

Jarboe thought a moment. "Put that way, yes."

Taff snorted. "Then get the meal out of your mouth."

Jarboe gave him a baleful glance, and started for the door again.

Taff said, "One more thing," and when Jarboe halted, Taff grinned. "This'll hurt the worst. Money."

Jarboe reached in his pocket and pulled out a worn, limp purse. Without looking at it, he tossed it to Taff, who caught it. Taff said dryly, "I'll need more than five dollars, R. B."

"There's two hundred in there," Jarboe said sardonically. "That ought to carry you through the day." He went out.

Taff leaned back in his chair and slowly pocketed the purse. He had the old man up a tree this time, he knew, and he tasted the pleasure of it. He'd run Jarboe's chores for him, had accepted his temper and his crotchets, his greed and his bullying for two years now. All the time he'd been watching the old man, and this morning, he finally had his true measure. The old man was flawed; he lacked the ultimate courage, and once a man understood that, he was Jarboe's master.

Now, with nothing to distract him, he gave close attention to the plan he had been turning over in his mind ever since yesterday. It had been a small thing that suggested it, but the more he thought of it, the more plausible it seemed.

That small thing had been the way Mrs. Storrs, when he and Hazeltine and Bishop had encountered her with Moffat in front of the hotel, had suddenly withdrawn her hand from Larkin Moffat's arm. It had suggested something specifically guilty to him, then, and he set about to review the supporting facts.

First, there was the fact that Charlie Storrs had said both he and Mrs. Storrs had known Moffat long ago. Then there was his memory of the way Mrs. Storrs had waited for Moffat to send her away when the fight in the hotel lobby started. Lastly, and most important, she and Moffat had gone downstreet together in the direction of Moffat's shack yesterday afternoon. And a blind man could have seen, as he did, that when Mrs. Storrs returned alone something of the deepest concern had upset her at Moffat's shack.

Did that add up to the fact that they had resumed an old love affair? It might, but he wished he had a little more evidence, anything that would wipe out his last lagging doubt. Once he had it, his scheme was foolproof. *Then get it*, he told himself. *You haven't much time.*

He went out, forcing a patience on himself. His first call, casual enough, was at the hotel, where he inquired if Mrs. Storrs was around. He was told she had left an hour or so ago. With her husband? No.

On the hotel steps, he pondered this. She couldn't kill an hour in this town, so she must be out of town. At Paxon's livery, he found she had rented a rig and gone for a drive. Alone, too.

He asked for his horse then and while it was being saddled, he stepped across the street to Beaufort's bunkhouse. Since he was an old hand at Jarboe's business here, his entrance went unremarked. After cruising a couple of aisles, he finally passed Arnie's bunk. Arnie was still in

93

it, had been in it ever since Moffat clouted him with the rock. That was good, too, he thought.

Picking up his horse at the livery, he rode south out of town and down the valley, and where the Big Jay road turned off the main road to Apex, he pulled off in the brush where he could watch both roads. He wondered with a patient fatalism which it would be.

He barely had time to smoke down a cigar when he heard the horse on the Big Jay road. When he saw the buggy, he stepped out of the brush, leading his horse, and halted by the side of the road.

Mrs. Storrs was driving the buggy. Bill raised a hand, and when the buggy halted beside him he touched his hat and said, "They're saying in town the Big Jay Road is blocked. Is that right, Mrs. Storrs?"

Josephine eyed him uncertainly, but there was no suspicion in her face. She was a beautiful woman, he thought impersonally, with the bland and placid self-confidence of all beautiful women. It covered their emotions like a mask made of cast iron, he reflected.

She smiled then and said, "I should say it is. I spent half an hour trying to turn this buggy around on the narrow road."

Bill said easily, "Well, it doesn't matter," and touched his hat again and stepped back.

Josephine drove on and Bill watched her a moment, a slow satisfaction stirring within him. That clinched it, and his scheme could go along now. If she had seen Moffat once without her husband, that could be written off as accident. Not this visit, though. He had what he needed.

His ride back to town was leisurely, and he felt pleased with himself. He was stabling his horse when the noon whistle at the mill blew, and he hurried a little.

Finished, he went down the street to the Comfort and went inside. The room was noisy with the men who had dropped in for a drink before dinner, and Taff moved to the bar.

He saw Charlie Storrs bellied up to the bar alongside Morton Dacy, and now Bill moved in beside Storrs.

Charlie turned to look at his neighbor, and when he saw Taff he laughed jovially. "If you can get a drink in that face of yours, Bill, I'll buy you one." He stepped

94

back. "You know Mort Dacy, the man whose claim I'm trying to steal?"

"I know Mort," Taff said, and he and Dacy shook hands across Storrs' midriff. Dacy was a middle-aged business man from Apex who speculated mildly in claims; now he looked at Charlie and said, "I wouldn't call it stealing. He hasn't pulled a gun on me—yet."

Charlie laughed, again jovially, and Taff supposed he and Dacy were coming to terms. Bill ordered his drink and looked at himself in the bar mirror. He agreed with Charlie; his swollen, bruised face was a sight, and now he thought sardonically, *For what I'm going to get out of this, I might as well let him add one more bruise.*

When his drink came, he asked for three cigars and passed them out. When they had fired up, Dacy brought up the question which Bill knew was inevitable. "Hear about the hard luck they had up at the Big Jay last night?"

Bill looked at his cigar and said mildly, "Why, yes. Mrs. Storrs said the road was blocked."

Charlie said immediately, "Mrs. Storrs? My wife? What does she know about it?"

"She tried to get up there this morning and couldn't."

Charlie scowled. "Good Lord! Don't tell me she got out of bed before noon."

"Way before," Bill said dryly.

"But what was she going up there for?" Charlie persisted.

"I suppose to see your friend. She didn't say."

"Moffat?"

"That's right."

There was an awkward pause, and Bill looked into the bar mirror. He could see Charlie scowling at him; Dacy was watching this closely, too.

Slowly, Bill wiped a palm over his mouth and glanced furtively, obliquely, at Charlie and then away. Then he shook his head and sighed. "Well, I talked out of turn, it looks like."

He looked full at Charlie and said, "I apologize," and turned to leave the bar.

Charlie Storrs grabbed him by the arm and halted him. "Just a moment," Charlie said grimly. "I don't know what this is all about, but I want to."

"Well, ask her, why don't you?" Taff said mildly.

"I don't mean that," Charlie said sharply. "Why do you think you talked out of turn?"

Bill said pleasantly, reasonably, "Look, let's forget this. How about it?"

Dacy said, "Well, see you later, Charlie," and shoved away from the bar. Dacy was ducking out, Bill knew, and he also knew other men were watching this, for talk around them was subsiding.

Charlie still had his arm, and he paid not the slightest attention to Dacy. He said, "I'm forgetting nothing. I want to know."

"Are you sure you do?" Bill prodded.

Charlie said with a hot anger, "Damn sure!"

Again Taff wiped his mouth, and he knew a dozen men were listening. "Well," he said resignedly, "I guess I talked out of turn because I didn't put two and two together."

"I don't get it," Charlie said curtly.

"Well, I saw her going into Moffat's shack with him yesterday afternoon," Bill said. "I figured you probably knew that. And then when I told you about her going up to see him this morning, I figured you knew about that, too. I didn't mean——"

Charlie hit him in the face then, and Bill saw it coming and rode the blow. But Charlie had been quick and Taff was off balance and he fell. He lay on his back a moment, and then raised up on one elbow. He looked at Charlie without rancor, and said, "Well, I apologize. I don't want any fight."

"You're a damned liar!" Charlie said wrathfully.

"All right," Bill said. "Only ask her." He came to his feet now and dusted off the seat of his trousers. There was a dead silence in the barroom now.

Charlie Storrs' broad face was flushed a deep red with anger. He opened his mouth to say something, and then, thinking better of it, he brushed past Bill Taff and headed straight for the door.

Bill waited until he had gone out, and then he shook his head slowly. He said plaintively, to the room, "Now if a man can't trust his wife, why don't he lock her in a room?"

96

He waited, and the laughs came, and now he was content. The whole town knew.

Josephine, from the window of their room, saw Charlie come out of the Comfort. She turned away from the window then, picked up her handkerchief from the dresser and looked briefly about the room. She might as well meet Charlie in the lobby. Before she left, however, she went over to the mirror and looked carefully at herself. She looked much as usual, she thought, with perhaps a little more color in her cheeks than normally, because of this morning's drive. There was nothing in her face that betrayed the tortured and sleepless night she had spent, nothing in her eyes to indicate the bitter regret she felt at having acted as she had yesterday toward Larkin. Nor was there any sign of the wild impatience that had been riding her since daylight, an impatience to see him again, to tell him she had been a fool and was bitterly sorry for it. It was far too late to try to persuade him she did not love him, because he knew better. All she wanted was a chance to prove her love.

Yet the woman she saw in the mirror was a pretty, placid-looking thing. *A cow*, she thought furiously, and turned away to the door, wondering why she should be angry that her face did not give her away. It was almost as if she had been conditioning herself for this moment since the day she married Charlie. The deception was too easy.

In the corridor, she raised her head slightly and caught the odor of boiled cabbage, from below, and she slowed her pace, half decided to pass up what was sure to be a foul-smelling dinner. But, strangely, she was hungry, and she went on, turning down the steps.

She saw Charlie then at the bottom of the stairs. He was taking the steps two at a time, with his usual disgusting ebullience, and he was halfway up them before he looked up and saw her.

Josephine said, "We might as well get it over with, Charlie. Let's eat."

Charlie's jaw was set grimly and he came on, one step at a time. When he came up to her, he took her elbow in his hand and said, "Turn around. Go back to the room."

A sudden panic touched Josephine, and was instantly gone. She said, "You're hurting me, Charlie. Let go." She looked searchingly at him. "What's got into you?"

Charlie gripped her arm harder, and Josephine tried to pull away. Implacably, Charlie turned her around, and she gave in, climbing the stairs beside him. She thought, *Does he know?* and immediately answered herself. *How could he?*

Charlie's grip did not relax until he opened the door to their room, and then he propelled her into it with a violence that half turned her around and sat her down on the bed. Josephine knew a faint thrust of fear; she had never seen Charlie this angry.

Charlie sailed his hat in the direction of the dresser and then confronted her, hands on hips.

"Now, sweetheart," he began ominously, "what have you been up to while my back's been turned?"

Josephine gave him a cool, appraising glance, and said dryly, "If you're trying to scare me, Charlie, you can stop. Now, what is it you want to know?"

"I just knocked down Bill Taff in the Comfort for insulting you."

"How brave of you," Josephine said. "What did he say, though?"

"You don't know?"

"I saw him when I was out driving this morning. Is there any connection?"

"Where were you driving?"

"To see Larkin," Josephine said calmly.

"Didn't you see enough of him at his shack yesterday afternoon?" Charlie asked with a savage sarcasm.

Something deep in Josephine warned her, *Taff told him. Don't lie to him,* and now she said calmly. "As a matter of fact I didn't. We quarreled, and I left."

Amazement crept into Charlie's angry face. "Quarreled?"

"About that Surrency girl. I teased him about her, and he got angry and so did I. I was going to see him this morning and apologize for a very childish piece of scolding."

Charlie didn't believe her, she saw, but for the moment he was mute, whether with astonishment or anger she didn't know. But she saw her advantage and she pressed it.

She said icily, "Why do you have to be such a gullible fool, Charlie? Why do you——"

Charlie made a swift, downswinging gesture with his hand that cut off her speech as effectively as if he had struck her. He came a step closer and said, "Did I ask you, or didn't I, to go with me yesterday afternoon?"

"You did, and I didn't want to go."

"So you could see Larkin instead?"

"Because those drives to mines bore me!" Josephine said angrily.

"But not a drive to the Big Jay," Charlie taunted.

Josephine fisted her hand and beat her knee with it. "But can't you see the difference? I wanted to tell Larkin I was sorry for what I'd said!"

"That's important," Charlie said dryly. "It's important to me that you care what he thinks. Why do you?"

Josephine sighed in exasperation. "I was just being *nice*," she said furiously. "It was just manners—something you wouldn't understand."

"I'm trying to understand why you bother to be nice to that crook," Charlie said heavily.

Josephine saw the importance of diverting him, and now she said scathingly, "Charlie, are you jealous of Larkin?"

"Good God! Should I be?"

"Then why are you acting this way?"

"I'm trying to tell you!" Charlie flared angrily. "You meet him twice behind my back. You——"

"Then come with me," Josephine said angrily. "The only reason I didn't ask you is because you're never here! You never pay any——"

"Oh, Lord!" Charlie groaned. "Here we go again. You're neglected!"

Josephine had her diversion. If she could get this quarrel removed from the particular to the general, it would bog down in a series of bitter and inconclusive accusations. She seized on this immediately and said, "All right, I'm neglected."

"Go home, then!"

"I'm neglected at home, too. Why should I go?"

Charlie stood there baffled, feeling swindled, wondering why they were talking about this and too angry to be logical. He took a deep breath, forcing a control upon himself, and said heavily, "Now, look. You——"

"I know," Josephine cut in acidly. "I'll never speak to Larkin again. When I see him, I'll spit in his face. I'll stay in my room and darn your socks. If anybody knocks on the door I'll hide under the bed. I'll——"

"Shut up!' Charlie bellowed.

"Louder," Josephine gibed.

Charlie stood there glaring at her, and Josephine knew she had blunted the edge of his anger. The immediate danger was over, she judged and she said, "Are you through scolding me for what some dirty-minded miner made up about me?" She rose. "Because if you are, I'm still hungry."

Charlie was still mad, but the wrath in his face was suffused with an expression of sullen frustration. Josephine skirted him slowly, opened the door, stepped out and closed it behind her.

She took the steps deliberately, this time, because her knees were weak and unsteady. Now that she was away from him, she realized this quarrel had settled nothing. Charlie was wildly jealous, and because it was Larkin Moffat of whom he was jealous, anything could happen, Josephine knew.

She came out into the lobby and looked over at Mrs. Barber, who, as she did every noon, was lying in wait to taunt her.

"Well, well," Mrs. Barber boomed. "Up bright and early this morning, weren't you? I'll bet you're hungry for once."

Josephine smiled gaily. "Oh, I am every day. Then I see the food."

When Josephine closed the door upon him, Charlie stood without moving for a full minute. Somehow, this was the way it always was; he felt he had been tricked. He had come into this room with the deepest grievance a man could hold toward a woman, and now all he had was cause for a mild sulk. What had happened? She hadn't evaded anything, hadn't lied, hadn't denied her guilt—but somehow she had contrived to make it not guilt. With that featherheaded woman's way of answering an argument, she had even left him with a feeling of guilt for having neglected her.

He swore bitterly, softly, and fisted his hands in his hip pockets and tramped over to the window, where he looked out upon the noon traffic. Without the distraction of anger, he went back carefully over everything she had said. Yes, she'd gone to Larkin's shack and yes, she'd tried to see him this morning because she had teased him into a temper about the Surrency girl. Remembering Josephine's several references to the Surrency girl, Charlie wondered, *Why did she tease him about her? Why does she care?* The answer to that question would be obvious to a man who knew only two females, he thought bitterly. *She's jealous of the Surrency girl.*

And if that were true, the rest of it was plain enough. She'd gone to Larkin because she wanted to be around him, *because she loves him.* Why not? They'd loved each other once, he remembered. A dismal sense of loss and be-wilderment was in Charlie for a moment. Josephine, be-cause she might be slipping away from him, was the most precious thing in the world to him in that instant.

He rubbed a hand slowly over his eyes, and down his nose and then he rubbed his mouth hard, pressing his lips against his teeth with the flat of his palm. There was a sensible way to look at this. Josephine was bored, and had turned to an old beau for excitement. Moffat, though, was another matter. If he'd take a bribe, he'd take a man's wife. The thing to do was make it plain to Moffat that he was to keep away from Josephine. From him, too. A once-bought man was no man, and Moffat might as well be told so.

Arrived at his decision, Charlie picked up his hat from where it had fallen on the floor and went out of the room. Downstairs, in the dining room, he saw that Josephine was seated at their table, his empty place opposite her.

Charlie walked through the dining room, nodding to his many new acquaintances, staring them boldly in the eye when they chose to look at him. He had done the right thing at the Comfort, and any real man here would agree.

Coming up beside Josephine, he put a hand on the back of her chair and said quietly, "I'm going out to see Larkin."

Josephine gave him a bitter, hostile glance. She hesitated, and then said, "If I told you not to, you'd think I was trying to protect him, wouldn't you?"

"So what are you telling me?" Charlie asked dryly.

"That you'll make an utter fool of yourself."

Charlie smiled without humor. "I'd rather do that than have you do it for me."

He waited, and when she turned away from him and began to eat, he straightened up and went out.

Candace looked in the flour crock and mentally calculated the number of biscuits Spence and two hungry men could eat for supper. The flour was not enough, she knew, and she went over to the clothes corner, took down an old jacket of her father's, and shrugged into it. From the cupboard she took a cup and started for the door, then checked herself and went back to the doorway of Spence's room.

"I'm going over to the Hostetters a minute, Spence. Everything all right?"

"Look," Spence said. "If I can sit up, I can walk, can't I?"

"Try it."

"I have." Spence grinned. "I'm going to get in some clothes and go out."

Candace laughed. "All right, but wait until Dad gets home, will you? You'd be too heavy for me to carry back."

"Nobody'll carry me back," Spence said flatly. "I feel fine."

Candace went out, and, closing the door behind her, breathed deeply of the chill afternoon air. The overcast seemed to be lowering hourly, she thought, and there would be new snow on the peaks when it cleared. She turned round the corner of the house and took the trail through the brush to the Hostetters tent. There was a new stack of logs on the other side of their clearing, and astraddle one of them was Tom Hostetter. With his drawknife he was peeling the log; a great pile of pine bark, almost flesh-pink on the underside, was strewn about him.

Smoke was coming from the pipe in the tent, and Candace halted at the flap and called, "Anybody home?"

"Come in," Martha Hostetter answered from inside,

and then she added, "Oh, no, Candace. It's easier for me to come out."

Candace heard a movement inside and the tent flap lifted and Martha Hostetter stepped out and straightened up. She was a worn-looking cheerful woman, under middle age, with a kind of raffish good humor in her face. "Honestly," she said, "if Tom doesn't get our place built soon, I'll be humpbacked from crawling around that tent." She saw the cup in Candace's hand. "Sugar, is it?"

Candace said it was flour, and Mrs. Hostetter took the cup and dived back into the tent. Tom Hostetter looked up from his work now and saw her and waved, and Candace waved back.

Mrs. Hostetter returned with the cup filled with flour. As she handed it to Candace, she asked good-humoredly, "Say, what kind of a ladies'——" She paused and looked alongside the tent. "Sadie around there?"

"I didn't see her."

Martha Hostetter grinned, and resumed her question. "What kind of a ladies' man has your father hired for a foreman, anyway?"

"Well, what kind has he?" Candace asked slowly.

"Tom was having a drink in the Comfort this noon when a fight started between Bill Taff and that new mining company man with the pretty wife, what's-his-name?"

"Storrs."

"Yes, at the hotel. I guess Taff let slip that he'd seen this Mrs. Storrs going to your man's shack, what's-his name?"

"Moffat?" Candace prompted, a kind of dread in her voice.

"Moffat, yes. Imagine. Storrs knocked him down for saying it, but it was true. Knocked down Taff, I mean. But your foreman, you want to be careful, Candace. Dutch ought to know it. He's handsome, too. Your foreman, I mean."

"Yes," Candace said dully. "I've got a cake in the oven, Martha. Thanks for the flour."

She turned, and walked around the tent, and she was conscious of a sick feeling inside her. This sordid, shabby story made a lie out of everything Larkin had told her. *It doesn't have to be true,* she told herself. If the story stemmed from Bill Taff, it could easily be malicious and a lie. But why would Taff risk a fight, even risk being killed by Charlie Storrs to spread an untrue story —and one that, as far as she could see, would not profit him?

As she approached the cabin she composed her face, so that Spence would notice nothing. But when she went inside, she found the place empty. Spence had dressed and was trying his legs on a walk somewhere.

Candace sank into one of the chairs and stared miserably at the table. When she had talked to him yesterday morning as he was chopping wood, Larkin had been serene and untroubled in the telling of his relationship with Josephine Storrs. He had talked with the open honesty of a man who had made a mistake in the past and was no longer bedeviled by it. She had even got it out of him, and she was still ashamed of it, that Josephine Storrs meant nothing to him any more. And now what was she to make of this slimy bit of gossip? Even if it was true, the mere fact that it was told about him somehow cheapened him.

She rose, not wanting to think about it and knowing she couldn't help it. She had planned on a big dinner tonight, a sort of party celebrating the fact that the rock slide had been no more serious than it was, and that the new ore chute would be completed today. Now, she had no heart for it. But she set grimly about the business of preparing the meal.

It was almost dark when she heard her father and Larkin ride up to the house. She heard one horse move on to the shed, while the other halted outside the door. Then the door opened, and she looked over her shoulder as Larkin stepped inside. He was smiling a little, as if he were looking forward to this evening too, and he said, "Hello, Candace," as he closed the door behind him and started toward her.

"Get it done?" Candace asked briskly, not looking at him.

"Done and working." He halted by the table, which was already set, fished a sour pickle out of the dish, and crammed it in his mouth.

Candace stole a glance at him; he seemed completely

104

natural, at ease. Now he spoke with his mouth full. "Can you use a half-deer, Candace?"

Candace looked up at him, her face as composed as she could make it. "Why, I suppose."

"Manahan is trying to make up to me for getting drunk. He offered me a half-deer." He smiled then, and Candace looked away.

"That would be nice," she said. No matter how hard she tried, she could not make her voice sound natural. This was the voice of a schoolteacher, professionally sweet, without warmth.

She glanced up at Larkin, wondering if he noticed it, and surprised him watching her, the start of a frown on his face. He said, "Have I time to get it before supper?"

"Lots."

She didn't look up until she heard the door close behind him, and then she paused in her work and drew a deep breath. Larkin already knew something was troubling her, and soon he would ask what it was. What was she to tell him, since she didn't know?

She hadn't answered that when Dutch came in. He slammed the door behind him, bringing in a gust of cold air, and when Candace looked at him he was rubbing his hands and smiling. "Lordy, Lordy, hurry up that food."

He came over and kissed her cheek, and she said, "Larkin says the new chute's working." She detected that same unnatural tone in her voice, and she hated it.

Dutch said, "This time it's guarded. So's the ore, and so's the slope above." He shucked out of his coat and prowled over to his room and looked inside. "Where's Spence?"

"Trying his legs, I guess. He slipped out while I was gone."

Dutch laughed and came over to the sink, rolling up his sleeves. He poured some hot water from the kettle into the washbasin and washed, then combed his hair and his beard. Candace moved quietly from stove to table to cupboard, and Dutch watched her in the mirror, taking an inordinate amount of time with the combing of his hair.

Candace was aware that the usual evening chatter,

105

the gossip of the mine and her quiet day, was lacking tonight, and she beat her mind frantically for something to talk about.

Dutch's quiet voice cut in on her thoughts, then. "Puss, what's troubling you?"

Candace was at the cupboard reaching for a dish when he spoke. Her hand paused for only a second, and then she got the dish and looked briefly at her father and said, "Why, nothing," in that artificial voice.

Dutch pulled a chair away from the table and sat down, and when she moved over to the stove, he said quietly, "Come on. What is it?"

"Nothing, I tell you," Candace exclaimed, almost with sharpness.

"Look at me," Dutch said.

Candace turned to look at him.

Dutch said, "You've been listening to gossip, haven't you? About Larkin."

Candace felt her face flushing, and with it came a curious defiance. "All right, I have."

"Ugly stuff, wasn't it?"

"What I heard was."

Dutch said mildly, "Do you care?" and regarded her carefully, watchfully.

That directness was typical of him, Candace thought; he was asking her an honest blunt question, and she knew exactly what he meant. She could pretend to misunderstand him, or she could evade an answer, or she could hide behind the right to her own privacy. Instead, she said soberly, "I've never cared more about anything, Dad."

Dutch tilted back in his chair and asked, "What did you hear?" and Candace told him. Dutch listened carefully, and when she was finished he said, "Maybe I can add to that. Storrs came up to the mine afterward. Larkin and I were having a smoke in the office when he came in. He was wild mad; he told me to leave, that he wanted to talk to Larkin."

"Did you?"

Dutch's beard moved in a smile. "Not exactly. I can tell when a man's killing-mad, and Larkin didn't have a gun. I moved around to the window on the other side of the office. When I got there Storrs was threatening to

106

kill him if he ever spoke to his wife again. Then Larkin asked him what this was all about."

"Hadn't Larkin heard about the fight in the saloon?"

"No. Storrs told him."

"What did Larkin say to that?"

"Larkin asked Storrs if he'd talked to Josephine," Dutch said. "Storrs said he had. He said *her* story was she'd gone to Larkin's shack and they'd quarreled over a woman."

"A woman?" Candace asked quickly. The old dread was here again.

"That's what Storrs said," Dutch answered dryly.

"What woman? Did he say?"

Dutch said levelly, "Yes. You."

The unexpectedness of her father's answer held Candace motionless while her mind tried to accept and evaluate this. A dozen implications invited consideration, but she was too confused, and what she felt was an odd and bewildering exultation.

Dutch said, "Aren't your biscuits burning?"

Candace wheeled and yanked open the oven door. With her apron for a holder she lifted out the pan of biscuits, and then without even noticing their condition, she slid the pan on the table and turned back to her father.

"Did Larkin admit this was true, Dad?"

"To every question Storrs asked him, Larkin always had the same answer—'What does Josephine say?' When Storrs would tell him, Larkin would say, 'Then that's what happened, Charlie.'"

"Was he just protecting her, Dad?"

"That's what Storrs thought."

"What do you think?"

"I think that's really what happened," Dutch said. "Afterwards Storrs threatened him again, told him to keep clear of his wife and himself or he'd shoot him. He cursed him, and threw the Corona business in his face. Larkin took this for a while and then he stood up and said, 'Charlie, the whistle's blown,' and walked out on him. So I think that's what happened."

Candace said gently, "Why do you, Dad?"

Dutch rose and said idly, "Maybe for the same reason you believe it, Puss. We both want to."

From five-thirty in the evening until some time around nine o'clock, Beaufort's bunkhouse was almost deserted. The bulk of its patrons, who worked the normal day shift in mine and mill, were eating or finding a rough fun at the bar and tables of the saloons.

So it was after six that Bill Taff, the pocket of his duck jacket sagging with its load of a bottle of whiskey, entered the bunkhouse, confident that it would be practically deserted.

He exchanged a good-evening with the old watchman and took the first aisle to his left. Tramping down it, he glanced at the bunks, and saw that an average of one bunk in thirty was tenanted at the moment.

As he approached Arnie's aisle, however, he was more careful. Looking in the bunks on both aisles flanking Arnie's aisle he found them deserted, and finally turned down the aisle he wanted. Even here, he cruised past Arnie, examining the bunks. When, at last, he was satisfied that nobody, not even a sleeping miner, was within earshot, he returned to Arnie's bunk and halted beside it in the half-light.

"Who's there?" Arnie asked.

"Taff. How you feeling, Arnie?"

"Not good," Arnie said sullenly.

"I can understand that," Bill said equably. "You're lucky Moffat left you a head." He sat down on the edge of the bunk across the aisle and, drawing out his bottle of whiskey, he uncorked it and extended it to Arnie. "How about some of the blessed stuff?"

"Sure," Arnie said, and took the bottle.

Bill watched him drink, and he wished there were more light here so he could see the man. He knew him well enough, though, that he thought he could trust the whiskey to have its usual effect. Sober, Arnie was a moody, troublesome miner who was almost always out of work because of his truculence with his fellow workers and bosses. In drink, he was a man other men avoided as they would the plague, for it was his invariable habit to dredge up old slights, fancied or otherwise, and when the whiskey turned them into grudges, he would erupt with a berserk fury. He had lost his job over the beating up of Spence Fuller, Bill knew, and he also knew he could not get another.

Arnie took a second, deeper drink from the bottle and extended it, and Bill said, "Go ahead." Arnie lay back in his bunk, the bottle on his belly and after a moment, Bill asked idly, "Going to pull out when you're all right again, Arnie?"

"I got no money to," Arnie said. "I got no job."

Bill, of course, had figured this; he reached in the pocket of his jacket and brought out Jarboe's work purse and tossed it onto Arnie's bunk. The sound it made when it landed was solid, musical as only gold coins can be musical. "Two hundred dollars," Bill said. "I'll have another two hundred for you when I meet you in Weed next week."

Arnie turned his head to look at him. "What's this for?"

"Take a drink."

Presently, Arnie did. This time he extended the bottle and Bill took it, and had a drink himself. He corked the bottle then and set it on the floor. Judging Arnie had got used to the idea of money by now, he said, "If I could do this job myself without hanging for it, I wouldn't come to you, Arnie." He paused. "I want Moffat out of the way."

"And I don't hang for it?" Arnie asked angrily.

"Another man does," Bill said. Without haste then, Bill described the situation between Moffat, Charlie Storrs, and Josephine Storrs, giving a graphic and earthy interpretation to it that Arnie could understand. Josephine was trash, Moffat a philanderer, and Charlie a bumbling fool, Taff said, neglecting to mention his part in maneuvering this situation. The whole camp knew, Bill said, that Moffat and Mrs. Storrs were lovers, and the whole camp knew that Charlie Storrs would like to kill Moffat. When Moffat was killed, the law would look for Storrs.

"But suppose Storrs can prove he never done it?" Arnie said.

"He can't tonight."

"Tonight?" Arnie raised up an elbow, peering at Taff. "Tonight?" he repeated.

"Why, yes," Bill said idly.

"But I'm sick."

"That's what protects you," Taff said easily. He

hitched forward, his voice lowering. "Look. Moffat's at Surrency's now. He'll likely spend the evening there. All you've got to do is pull on a pair of pants, cut a hole in the canvas back here so you won't go past the watchman, climb down the logs, and go to Surrency's. Once the job's done, come back here, climb back into your bunk, and nobody's missed you."

Arnie was silent. Taff picked up the bottle and extended it, and Arnie took it and drank and handed it back, all without speaking. Then he said, "This Storrs, where'll he be?"

"I'll get him out of town with a note. I know he'll go, and he'll be alone. You won't even leave here till I'm sure of that."

He waited, and Arnie was silent. Then Arnie lay back in his bunk, staring at the bunk above him. Bill went on, "They'll be after me first, because they know I'd like to kill Moffat. But I'll be in the Comfort the whole night. Then they'll think of Storrs. He'll have been waiting down at the bridge alone to see the man who wrote him the note."

"What note?" Arnie asked.

"The note I send to him," Bill said, patiently. "The note that will tell him if he really wants to find out about Moffat and his wife, he'd better be waiting at the bridge tonight."

There was a long pause, while Arnie thought this over.

"Show me a hole in it," Taff said.

Still Arnie didn't answer. Taff spread his hands. "Once they've got Storrs, I ride over to Weed, pay you the rest of the money, and you drift. Show me a hole in it," he repeated.

Arnie sighed. "I sure need the money," he said meditatively. "I sure could use some."

6

IT WAS WHEN the supper clean-up was over with and Candace had taken off her apron that Moffat, Dutch, and Spence sought chairs around the table; Moffat watched Candace do the day's last chore. She took the ball of sourdough starter left over from the biscuits, put it in a small pan, poured potato water into it, stirred some flour in, set the pan on top of the warming oven, and put a cloth over it. Her movements were careless and expert; Moffat watched her contentedly until she went over to the mirror to smooth back her pale hair, and then he tamped down the coal of his pipe, wondering again at the change that had come over her between the time he had first seen her this evening and when he returned from Manahan's.

Dutch rolled the half-length of cigar across his mouth, and then removed it, looking at Candace. He said, "Candace, let's count our money tonight."

Candace said without turning, "That's bad luck, isn't it, Dad?"

"They can't steal the ore we've got out. You got paper around here? I want to figure."

Candace moved toward her room, and now Spence cocked an ear and said presently, "What's the racket in the shed?"

They all listened, and then Dutch rose, saying, "Likely the smell of blood from that deer has got the horses nervous. I better move it."

Spence said, "Deer? Who's had time to hunt?"

Dutch, moving toward his coat, told him of Manahan's gift and now Spence rose too, saying, "If Manahan killed that deer, it must have been with a whiskey bottle. Let's see it."

Dutch took down the lantern and lighted it and he and Spence stepped out into the night, closing the door behind them. Moffat only stirred faintly, contentedly, listening to Candace move about her bedroom. In a moment she came out with paper, pen, and ink and set them on the table, by the lamp, and then she looked at Moffat with a conspirator's smile.

"I wondered how long Dad could hold out."

Moffat said, "He's held out longer than I would have," and watched her sit down. He said then, looking down at his pipe, "Candace, what was the trouble this afternoon?"

She glanced up at him, startled, and saw him watch-

111

ing her. He knew she was pondering an evasion and rejecting it, and finally she only shook her head shyly and remained silent.

"Was it talk of me and Josephine that upset you?"

"Why, I heard talk," Candace said guardedly.

"And you believed it?"

Candace said, "Well, she's pretty."

Moffat scowled. "Is she any prettier now than when I told you she meant nothing to me?"

"I wouldn't be surprised."

A frank astonishment mounted in Moffat's face, and he said, "Now, how do you figure that?"

"They say a woman in love is more beautiful than ordinary."

Moffat leaned forward now, folding his arms on the table, and they regarded each other closely for a long moment. Moffat said then, "Candace, what have you been hearing?"

"It's not what I've been hearing, it's what I've been thinking."

"And what is that?"

"That a married woman is never such a fool as to risk her reputation unless she can't help herself, unless she is in love."

"And I'm to blame for that?"

Candace shook her head gently, in negation. "In no way."

"But you believed the talk," Moffat persisted.

"That much of it, yes; that she went with you to your place."

"I'm trying to see why it upset you, if you believed what I told you."

Candace gave him a strange, lingering look and then said dryly, "Why, maybe it's because what she said is true. That I'm after you too."

Moffat said sharply, "How do you know she said that, Candace?"

Candace rose abruptly, and there was the shadow of anger in her dark eyes. "Oh, I don't, Larkin. There's nothing much that one woman can hide from another. I could guess what she said and I'm not thanking you for making me say it. Why do you care whether or not I believed it?"

112

Moffat rose too, and they looked searchingly at each other before he spoke. "I guess I don't care what anybody else *but* you thinks, Candace."

They both heard the voices of Spence and Dutch as they approached the door. Moffat, still looking intently at Candace, turned and moved toward the open woodbox, knocking the ashes from his pipe into his palm. Candace sat down slowly, pushing the paper and ink toward her father's chair as the door opened. She was trembling, Moffat saw. As he leaned over the box, dumping the dottle from his pipe into it, he was wondering greatly at his own last words. Yes, he had told her the plain truth; he wanted her to think more than well of him, and he was only now reading himself as he should have read himself before.

He straightened, and turned, his gaze seeking out Candace. She had leaned an elbow on the table, not looking at him, listening to Dutch say, "That's an awful little deer for that big a drunk."

Spence said, "A bull elk wouldn't fit one of Manahan's bats."

Moffat smiled absently, and teetered on his heels, back to the stove. He watched Dutch come over to the chair and seat himself, and then say, "Well, Larkin. Let's see how our guesses jibe."

Moffat pocketed his pipe, and was already in motion toward the table when he heard the gunshot outside. He was at the same time aware of two other things—the angle of a broken windowpane, and the firm touch of something on his lower neck where it joined the shoulder. It was the touch of a bullet.

In motion already, he lunged past the table toward the door, as Dutch came to his feet, overturning his chair. Moffat pulled his gun from its holster, opened the door with his left hand, and wheeled to his left out of the door, already running.

Past the corner of the house, he hauled up, gun at ready, listening. Above the sound of Dutch pounding out the door, he heard the crashing of brush beyond the stable, and he ran again in that direction.

Beyond the stable, he was halted abruptly by a tangle of thicket and he fell into it. Rising, he listened again, and again from the north came the sound of crashing brush.

It was a man afoot, Moffat judged, and backing out of the brush, he cursed silently at his lack of knowledge of the creek bottom here. Slowly, his vision was adjusting itself to the darkness. Bent low, so as to skyline the trees and avoid them, he ran on, and presently came to a trail of sorts. He stopped here, and ahead of him, perhaps a little to the right now, came the same blind trampling in the brush. *He's lost too,* Moffat thought, and he plunged on down the trail. Farther on, something solid slashed at his shins, and he tripped and fell heavily. Lying there, he listened again; and there was silence; then he came quietly to his feet. The night was still.

And then faintly, almost inaudibly, came a slow, rhythmic coughing, and for a moment Moffat listened, puzzled, and then it came to him. His assailant had halted too, and what Moffat was hearing was the labored breathing of the man. *How far?* Moffat wondered, and because he could not afford to let the man remain silent, he raised his gun, and shot blindly in the direction of the sound.

On the heels of the shot, his man was off again, and Moffat drove through the thicket. Branches tore at his clothes and his face as he bulled his way blindly deep into the thicket.

When he was where he judged his man had last stopped, he too halted. He could hear nothing for a moment over his heavy breathing, and then he picked up a new sound. It was the pounding of a man running on sod, and it came from ahead of him.

He plunged on again, knowing his man had broken clear of the brush and was heading frantically back toward the main street. And now for the first time, he let himself speculate on who the man might be. He was no woodsman, Moffat knew, for a man versed in outdoor ways would have trusted the darkness and his own immobility to hide him. *Charlie Storrs?* Moffat thought, and then it was out of his mind as he broke clear of the thicket.

He halted again, breathing through his mouth, so that the sound of his own heavy breathing was dimin-

114

ished, and he listened, and immediately picked up the sound of a man running.

Moffat broke into a run then, and he could see the lights of the main street up the slope ahead of him. If his man was aiming for the anonymity of town, the thing to do was to cut him off.

He aimed straight up the slope for the street and time and again, he was forced to skirt thickets, and once a dark cabin. His legs dragged heavily in protest against the uphill pace. Once, halting for breath he heard a movement off to his left, and he was almost even with it, and he drove on.

Now he had to swing left to miss the slab compound of a Petersen's freight lot, and he hefted his gun, calculating that his shift would put him close to his man.

Pulling clear of the compound, he saw he was in the rear of Holland's Survey Office, with Paxton's lantern across the street dimly skylining the road. Bending down close to the ground, he could see no one framed against the nimbus of the lanternlight.

He listened, carefully, then, trying to pick up the sound of his man against the night noises of the town. He could not, and he rose, puzzled, and glanced briefly at Beaufort's bunkhouse. Had his man been alarmed at the closeness of his pursuit and, seeing he would be cut off from town, turned back at the very road and retreated north? Moffat doubted it, and he moved across the vacant lot toward the bunkhouse.

Perhaps his man was hiding among the piles of the foundation here. But a cursory examination revealed nothing, and Moffat stood motionless by the pilings, baffled.

And then it came to him with a sudden jolting conviction. His man was in Beaufort's bunkhouse.

He wheeled and lunged up the hill to the street, and he was thinking. *That will be friend* Arnie. Only now did his anger override his stubbornness. He tramped through the door and saw the watchman seated at his post.

Moffat gestured with his gun and said, "Come on, Pop, and bring the lantern."

Something in his tone brought the old man to his feet. "Trouble? Not in here."

"Did Arnie come in here?"

"No."

"Bring your lantern," Moffat repeated stubbornly. He waited for the old man to pick up his lantern, and he hurried ahead of him along the head aisle and turned at the third passage to his left.

The lantern behind him cast his shadow huge and elongated down the aisle ahead of him. Hefting his gun he hurried the last few paces and halted at Arnie's bunk.

It was empty. He counted back from the rear wall to make sure, and then he looked up at the watchman.

"Is there a back door here?"

"No way out or in except past me," the watchman said dryly.

Moffat reached out and took the lantern from him and walked back to the rear wall. Raising the lantern, he looked up to where the logs met the canvas, and started to walk toward the corner.

And then he saw it—the long slash in the canvas where the rear wall met the sidewall. Arnie had climbed up the log butts and got inside; then, hearing Moffat's entrance he had climbed out again.

Moffat dropped the lantern, wheeled and raced past the watchman for the head aisle. Rounding it, he collided with a man, and did not even stop to explain. Shouldering past, he raced out the door, turning downstreet.

And there, almost at the four corners, he saw a man running down the road. He started to raise his gun and knew it was useless, and he ran hard.

Arnie was at the Comfort by now, and he looked back over his shoulder. Then he was lost for a moment among the horses racked at the Comfort's tie rail, but only for seconds. Then Moffat saw him swing astride a horse, wheel it into the street, and head down it. Someone on the hotel steps shouted.

Moffat shot wildly, running still, and when he was at the Comfort, he glanced quickly at the horses. Selecting the biggest horse, a bay, he untied him, swung him around, and put him downstreet in pursuit.

As Charlie Storrs, riding a horse from Paxton's livery, approached the bridge, he reined in and listened a moment, but the brawling of Bone Creek smothered the other night sounds with its racket. A faint uneasiness was in Charlie, and he wished he knew what he was getting into. The note had been delivered to him in the dining room by some ragged kid whom he did not think to question until after he'd gone and could not be called back. He had read the note and quietly pocketed it, and Josephine showed no interest. The import of the note, unmistakably enough, had sickened him, then; the thought of it sickened him now, too. Somebody else besides Taff had seen Josephine go with Moffat to his shack, and somebody else knew more than Taff about what happened there.

Charlie felt a touch of dread now as he put his horse in motion. He didn't want to hear what this man would tell him, yet he couldn't bear it if he didn't. He wondered bitterly who the man was, and how much he had already talked. He accepted with a gray fatalism the fact that he might presently hear the words that would pull his whole life to pieces and destroy his marriage. For, with the receipt of this note, he was absolutely convinced of Josephine's guilt.

There was nobody at the bridge when he slowly rode across it and reined up, peering around in the night. The bridge was without rails, only flat hewn logs stretching from one timber abutment to the other that bridged the narrow, deep Bone.

Charlie glanced down at the water. Perhaps the man he was to meet was hiding around the abutments, waiting for some sign of recognition.

Charlie called loudly, "It's all right. Come out."

Nobody answered, and he felt faintly foolish. There was nobody here. Because he supposed his informant would come from town, he crossed back to the other bank, dismounted, and tied his horse to some wayside brush.

Slowly, then he paced down to the bridge, crossed it, turned and paced back, his thoughts bleak and dismal. Supposing what he would learn tonight solidly confirmed his beliefs, what should he do? Leave Josephine? Kill Moffat?

He thought of this with pleasure, feeling the old anger mount. At his meeting with Moffat this afternoon, he had nearly done just that. The only thing that had

117

restrained him had been Moffat's quiet refusal to be baited—that, and a lingering suspicion that maybe Josephine might be telling the simple truth.

A sound in the night intruded, and he raised his head. Above the clamor of the Bone, he could hear a horse being ridden at a hard gallop, and the sound came from the direction of town. He walked quickly to his horse, listening. The sound continued for some while passing along down the creek behind him, and finally faded. Someone in a hurry had left the road for the trail to Weed that followed the Bone downstream a way, then took off for the peaks. Charlie sighed, miserable, and resumed his pacing.

He had scarcely reached the bridge again when the sound of a galloping horse came to him again. He halted and turned, curious, and soon he knew this horse was coming for the bridge. Perhaps this was his man, *and in a hell of a hurry*, he thought morosely.

He was standing beside his horse then when the bulk of the rider loomed in the night, coming headlong for the bridge.

And then the rider caught sight of him, and reined in savagely, swerving his horse toward Charlie. Charlie stepped back and the horse halted and a voice, only vaguely familiar but wicked with anger, said, "Who's that? Speak up!"

"Storrs," Charlie said.

The rider leaned down and now wiped a match alight on his leg, and Charlie saw Moffat. He was bareheaded, his face grim with anger, and Charlie had a fleeting feeling of guilt which he couldn't explain.

Moffat said wickedly, "Did a rider pass you, Charlie?"

"No."

The match died, and Moffat said sharply, "You're lying." He swung out of the saddle, and ducked under the head of his horse with a swiftness that surprised Charlie.

"Who were you meeting out here, Charlie?" Moffat demanded.

"My business," Charlie said curtly, anger stirring anew.

He felt Moffat reach out for his coat front, felt it balled up in Moffat's fist, and Moffat said, still sharply, "Think, Charlie. Did a rider pass you here?"

"I told you," Charlie said. And then he remembered the sound of the other horse. "A horse passed behind me a few minutes ago, on the Weed trail."

"Ah," Moffat said. "That's better." He let go of Charlie's coat, and stood motionless a moment, and then he said thinly, "That better be it, Charlie."

"Why had it?" Charlie demanded truculently.

"Arnie took a shot at me tonight," Moffat said savagely. "I hope you weren't meeting him. But I'll find out."

He didn't wait for Charlie to protest, but asked, "Is that one of Paxton's horses?"

"Yes."

"I'm taking him," Moffat said. "Take my horse and tie him in front of the Comfort. I borrowed him."

Without waiting for Charlie's answer, he moved over to untie the reins of Charlie's horse, and stepped into the saddle.

Charlie found his voice, then. He said bluntly, "If I wanted to shoot you, I wouldn't buy it done, my friend."

"We'll see," Moffat said, and he rode off up the road where he could pick up the trail.

Standing in the night, Candace saw Dutch circle fruitlessly once more in the brush and then, holding the lantern in front of him, head back through the thicket for the trail. Beyond, she could hear Spence, his lantern almost obscured from sight by the density of the thicket.

She stood there rigidly, dreading each second anew, waiting for a call from her father or Spence that they had found Larkin. And then she thought, *That's nonsense. If the killer couldn't hit him through the window, how could he hit him in the dark?*

Dutch was returning. Pulling out of the brush, he straightened up and looked silently at Candace. "I can't make out any tracks. But I'll bet that shot we heard was his."

Candace nodded, and then asked, "Who was it, Dad? Charlie Storrs?"

"It could be," Dutch said grimly. "It could be Taff, too, but I don't think Taff wants to hang that bad."

For an instant, Candace felt an almost uncontrollable

fury at Josephine Storrs. Charlie Storrs didn't count; he was only being used in a way he couldn't help.

Dutch called to Spence now, and then said to Candace, "I'm going up to town and look around."

"So am I," Candace said, with a promptness that surprised her.

Dutch said without conviction, "This is no time for a girl to be on the streets," and looked curiously at her.

"It's no time for propriety, either," Candace retorted.

She turned and started back for the house. Entering, she glanced at the window through which the shot had come, and again she wondered by what miracle the bullet had missed Larkin.

She took down a blanket coat from a nail in the corner and put it on, and was waiting silently when Dutch came in. He halted in the doorway and said, "You're set on this? Where are you going?"

"To the hotel."

Dutch gave her a strange look and said, "All right. Come on."

Spence was in the side yard, hunting the place from which Larkin's assailant had shot, and Dutch called to him where they were going.

Afterward, they took the trail through the alder thicket, Dutch with his lantern, leading the way. Candace walked in silence, pondering what she was to say to Josephine Storrs. When they passed Hostetters, Candace saw the orange lamp glow inside the tent, and she thought guiltily of her conversation with Martha Hostetter this afternoon. Perhaps she had believed more of Martha's gossip than she acknowledged to Larkin tonight. She remembered Larkin's words to her when they were alone this evening, and she held that memory close and private, treasuring it in an absurd way. Perhaps his words had been ordinary enough; but it was what she felt he was about to say before they were interrupted that excited her as she thought of it.

The town, as always after dark, had been taken over by men. They wandered aimlessly about the street, moving between the two saloons, using the middle of the road for meeting places as often as the scarce plank-walk. Many of them were not sober, Candace saw, and the din from the Silverbell's piano was more pathetic than tawdry.

Dutch left her at the door of the hotel, and she saw him cross back toward the Comfort before she went in. A scattering of men were loafing in the lobby, beginning their curious vigil for the stage which would bring them nothing and take them nowhere but which would satisfy their obscure longing for a contact with the outside world.

There was nobody behind the desk. Candace opened the register and found the number of the Storrs' room, and then she headed for the stairs. Mounting them, she had a fleeting moment of indecision which was soon gone.

Her knock was answered by Josephine, who opened the door. She was in a wrap, and her dark hair was combed out so that it fell deeply behind her shoulders. She had a book in her hand, and when she saw Candace a look of surprise crossed her face before her features settled into wariness.

Candace said, "May I come in?"

Josephine silently stepped aside, and Candace walked into the room. Josephine closed the door behind her, and the two women looked at each other levelly, the hostility between them almost palpable.

Candace said, "Your husband isn't here, Mrs. Storrs?"

"No. He had to go out," Josephine said slowly. She was trying, Candace saw, to guess the meaning of this visit.

"You don't know where?"

"He didn't say." Josephine was silent a moment, watching Candace closely. "Why do you want him?"

"Someone just shot through the window at Larkin Moffat."

The book Josephine had been holding at her side suddenly fell to the floor. She didn't look at it; her glance was steady and unblinking and terrible with uncertainty as she watched Candace's face. She asked hesitantly, fearfully, "Was he hurt?"

"I don't know. I don't think so."

The naked relief that came to Josephine's face was something that could not be hidden, and which she did not even try to hide. She took a deep shuddering breath, and then dragged her glance away from Candace. Her attention seemed to center on the book at her feet, and she gazed at it stupidly a moment, as if she had never seen it before. Then she said, without looking at Candace, "Was it Charlie?"

"That's what I came to find out," Candace said coldly.

"No," Josephine said flatly, and she looked up now. "It wasn't Charlie. He wouldn't do that."

"He threatened Larkin this afternoon."

A fit of trembling seized Josephine. She clasped her hands together and half turned away from Candace, and Candace could see the rigidity of her fingers as she tried to stop shaking.

Candace felt no pity for her, and a steadily mounting anger pushed her into speech. "Why don't you leave?" Candace said bluntly. "Haven't you done enough harm, without getting Larkin killed?"

Josephine wheeled on her and said swiftly, "Don't say that!"

"And why not?" Candace asked angrily. "If your husband kills him, whose fault will it be?"

"Charlie didn't try to kill him, I tell you!"

"When you've humiliated him in front of the whole town? When he's out of his mind with jealousy? When he's threatened already to do what he tried to do to-night?"

Josephine shook her head in denial, and said dismally, pleading in her voice, "But I've given him no cause for jealousy."

"You lie," Candace said flatly. "Not the cause he suspects, but another one. You're in love with Larkin, aren't you?"

Josephine held a sullen silence, and now Candace said implacably, "If you do love him, then why don't you leave?"

"So you can have him?" Josephine said bitterly.

"So Charlie won't kill him!"

Josephine's eyes were wholly dark with bitterness and she turned slowly to the window and looked out. Then she looked obliquely at Candace. "You love him, too, don't you?"

"Yes. I want him to live. Don't you?"

Josephine didn't answer, only turned her head away to look again at the night. She was silent an intolerable while, and Candace wondered what her thoughts could be. Slowly, almost imperceptibly, Josephine straightened up, and when she turned her head Candace saw the opaqueness of her eyes, the hardness of her mouth.

"Get out of here," Josephine said coldly.

Candace knew she had lost, knew that nothing could penetrate the armor of this woman's selfishness. Nothing short of Larkin's death would do that. She went out quietly, hating her.

Josephine listened intently to the fading sound of Candace's footsteps, and then turned and came back to the bed and sat on the edge of it. She stared with a kind of vacuous concentration at the book she had dropped on the floor. The cold touch of fear was still upon her. Now, she lay back on the bed, eyes open, staring at the ceiling, and she morosely considered this news. In spite of her denial to that Surrency girl, she knew it had been Charlie who tried to kill Larkin. He had come back from seeing Larkin at the Big Jay in a surly, silent temper. The note he had received but not shown her, at supper tonight, had only deepened his taciturnity, and he had left without a word to her. Something had pushed him to the decision, and tonight he had tried to kill Larkin. She hated Charlie then with an insensate bitterness, and beyond that lay a naked fear.

What was she to do now? If Charlie had tried to shoot Larkin and failed, would he dare to show himself now? She tried to recall everything Candace had told her about the attempt, and remembered only that Candace seemed not quite certain that it had been Charlie who shot. Then if he weren't seen, he would be back—and he would try again for Larkin.

Josephine shrewdly calculated her powers over Charlie. The sum was pitifully small and inadequate to keep him from trying until he killed Larkin. Now, any appeal to his love for her he would laugh at, she knew. Nor would the threat to his career be a matter of concern. *But somehow, some way, I must stop him,* she thought frantically. If he killed Larkin, she did not want to live herself.

She rose, a nameless dread in her, and began to pace

the room. Perhaps Larkin would kill him. Perhaps to-night, even now, Charlie was dead. No, that was absurd, because no problems in life were solved that easily.

She knew she was feverish, and she lay down on the bed, a kind of apathy upon her. The night noises outside were magnified; she found herself listening intently, waiting for something she couldn't name to happen.

It was some time later when she picked up the sound of footsteps almost the instant they left the lobby and began to mount the stairs. She listened, her breath held, and heard the steps reach the stairhead, turn, and come down the corridor. It was Charlie. She rose, and the bed was between her and the door when Charlie stepped in.

His face was sullen and heavy as he caught sight of her, and without a word he closed the door behind him. Josephine felt a wild wrath in her now; guilt seemed to be stamped in his face, in his every movement.

He halted now, regarding her distantly, and threw his hat on the bed. "What's happened to you?" he asked.

"That Surrency girl was here," Josephine said, her voice shaking with anger. "She told me about the shot at Larkin."

"Pity it missed," Charlie said dryly.

He knows, Josephine thought wildly. *He shot at him.* An uncontrollable rage seized her then and she cried, "You fool! You criminal, wicked fool!"

Charlie looked up, his attention sharp, as Josephine skirted the bed and came toward him.

"Did you think you could hide it from me? Did you think you could come back to me with his blood on your hands!"

She came at him furiously, raising both fisted hands above her head and beating with them at his chest and face.

With an almost contemptuous movement, Charlie grasped her wrists and held them. She struggled helplessly for seconds, her face twisted into ugliness with her anger and hatred of him. Then he shoved her away from him, and as she staggered back the bed caught her behind the knees and she sat down heavily.

Behind her anger, Josephine noticed Charlie's face was oddly bland, without passion, and it only heightened her anger.

124

He said in a mocking voice, "This is Larkin you're talking about, is it?"

Josephine was utterly reckless, without mind or caution, and her voice had climbed into an ugly high register as she shrilled, "If you hurt him, Charlie, I'll kill you, I'll see you hang! I'll dance on your tombstone!"

Charlie said nothing for a moment. His long brooding look at her seemed almost impersonal, as if he were looking at something inanimate that stirred only a mild curiosity in him. Then he said, "Well, I know now," and, a moment later, "I don't need to wonder any more, do I?"

Josephine watched him, not understanding his calmness and not wanting to. She watched him rub the back of his neck with his hand, and then sigh.

"Sweetheart," he said with a tired gentleness, "I didn't shoot at Larkin. Arnie Somebody did. Larkin told me. The whole town knows it—except you."

Josephine even then did not wholly understand this; she was becoming absorbed in the grim weariness of Charlie's voice and his movements. They were the voice and the movements of a man who had irrevocably settled something in his mind. Only slowly did the significance of what he had just said penetrate her mind, and when she grasped it, she felt nothing. She had betrayed her love for Larkin in the plainest way possible. Nothing she could do or say would redeem her, and she didn't care.

Charlie reached in his hip pocket now and brought out his purse and tossed it on the bed beside her.

"There's money. Go home. I don't want to see you any more. Just get away from me," Charlie said tiredly.

He turned and went out, closing the door behind him. Josephine looked a long time at the purse, and finally put her hand out to take it.

Charlie went heavily down the steps into the lobby. He looked blankly at the scattering of loungers and wandered out to the front steps where he halted.

The night was crisp and clear; the clouds had made only a threat and passed. He put his hands in his hip pockets and looked over the street. Suddenly, a feeling of unutterable misery came to him, and some deep animal instinct urged his body into motion, as if in movement he might lose the feeling. He walked down the

125

steps, and turned upstreet and crossed the sidestreet, hunting, by instinct again, the dark outskirts of the camp.

He had had the small satisfaction of ending this himself, of saying the last weary word, and now the door was shut. Josephine's revelation, bald and total, had nullified everything that had been good in their lives these last three years. It seemed to him now that Larkin Moffat had, in a way, only leased him Josephine's affections for those years. Larkin had had them once and discarded them; now he had them again, simply for the asking. His anger at Moffat, sore and deep and sustained, was something almost tangible then.

He passed Paxton's livery and soon the road petered out in a narrow wood road knifing into the timber, and Charlie walked slowly, welcoming the darkness around him. Presently, he came to a windfall beside the road and sat on it. He could hear the Bone below him thrashing its hurried way down out of the high country, and it reminded him of his fruitless wait at the bridge for the anonymous informer. It really didn't matter now what the writer of the note could tell him. He thought of Moffat then, and of how calmly he had appropriated his horse. *A wife or a horse,* Charlie thought grimly; *if he wants it he takes it.*

He hoped, with a quiet malevolence, that Arnie would trap Moffat and kill him. And even as the thought came to him, he straightened a little in the night. Kill Moffat? No, the man was too lucky, and Arnie obviously a fumbler. But suppose Moffat was killed tonight? The whole town knew he'd taken after Arnie with intent to kill, because Arnie had shot at him. Suppose he didn't come back and, days later, his body was found up in the mountains. Wouldn't the camp assume that this Moffat's luck had run out, and that Arnie had got him?

Charlie rose, a slow excitement stirring within him, and now he considered this with close care. Moffat had taken the trail to Weed, and he'd have to return by that trail. *Simple enough, for a man with patience,* Charlie thought. The whole history of his acquaintance with Moffat ribboned through his mind in fleeting bitter memory, then, galling him into his decision. He turned back toward Vermilion, and this time he walked purposefully.

126

Where the trail left the creek bottom to lift out of the valley of the Bone toward the peaks, Moffat found what he wanted. A seep had muddied a stretch of the trail here, and he dismounted. With the aid of matches, he carefully looked over the prints left in the mud, and when he found a clear set of tracks made by the last horse traveling east, he studied them, memorizing them.

Afterward, he lengthened his stirrups, for there was a long ride, and a cold one, ahead of him, he knew. Untying the slicker from his cantle, he donned it, and then mounted again, putting his horse in motion. His mount seemed fresh and willing, which was fortunate, because Arnie, he knew, was heading out of the country, and in his haste he had selected the hardest way.

This was undoubtedly a fool's errand, Moffat thought wryly. A sensible man, thankful to be alive and content in the knowledge that Arnie would never return, would call it quits at this point and go home. *But I am not a sensible man,* he thought grimly. A man in anger was entitled to shoot at him, but not through a window and not at his back. If wanting to kill that man was foolish and stubborn, so be it, he thought. Beyond that, however, there were other and better reasons for going ahead with this. Things needed explaining at this point. For instance, what was Charlie Storrs doing at the bridge, if not waiting for Arnie? And why had Arnie, sick and hurt as he was, waited until now to make his try? And if Bill Taff had paid Arnie once, couldn't he pay him again?

The answers lay with Arnie. Moffat shifted in his saddle, settling into patience, and he speculated idly on Arnie's probable movements tonight.

Arnie, knowing he was pursued, would ride hard. But once he left the timber for the snowy reaches of the boulder fields at the pass, he might lose heart. He too, Moffat remembered, was not dressed for this ride, and the pure misery of cold might drive him into framing an ambush this side of Bone Peak. Reckoning the danger, Moffat smiled faintly. If Arnie couldn't hit his lamplit back through a window, he couldn't hit him in darkness.

The trail broke out of the timber now into a meadow that was faintly touched by the light of the new moon in the west. Across the meadow he saw the white flags of several deer move off into the woods, and then the trail ducked into aspens, again climbing. Once again he dismounted at a soggy stretch of trail and checked for Arnie's tracks, and found them.

Two hours later, he had left timberline behind him and was in today's thin snow, where Arnie's tracks were plain. An insistent wind filtered down off the peaks from which his stiff slicker could not protect him, and he shivered miserably. At the boulder-strewn pass itself, the wind blew steadily and relentlessly, driving the new snow before it. Its force, though, had scoured the rocks almost bare of snow, and Moffat's horse took advantage of the good footing to hurry across.

Afterwards, when he was down to timberline on the far slope, he stopped and built a fire and, warm again, rode on.

Toward daylight, he was approaching the gravel buttes above Weed, and the tracks of Arnie's horse were still the freshest on the trail.

Moffat considered what was before him. Arnie might not stay in Weed, but he would have to stop there. His horse, unless fed and rested, would play out on him shortly. Too, there was food and whiskey in Weed, both of which Arnie would need.

So, just after daylight, when Moffat came out on one of the buttes above Weed and looked down at the sorry, rotting ghosts of the camp, he reined in and dismounted and studied the place. The clear, almost translucent morning air was utterly still; he could hear a dog barking, and the smoke from the store lifted string straight from its chimney, seeming to hold the circular shape of the stove pipe for a hundred feet before it scattered and vanished. There was no movement on the single street.

Shucking out of his slicker, Moffat loosened the cinch and slipped the bridle of his horse and turned him loose in the brush along the stream. But instead of following the trail along the steeply dropping stream bed, Moffat struck out across the buttes, preferring to approach the place from another direction.

Some minutes later he was among the tangle of sheds and the corral behind the store, and he hauled up here, looking at the rear of the store. There was a single window in the second story, a closed door below it, and a

128

window to the right of the door. If Arnie wanted food, this was the only place in Weed he could get it.

Smoke was coming from a single shack far down the road Moffat saw, and he watched it a moment, and then his attention turned to the store again. Arnie couldn't be sure he'd been followed, but he would be careful enough to prepare for it in case he was. Probably he would be watching the trail, where it turned away from the stream at the head of the street.

Moffat pulled his gun and hefted it, and then stepped clear of the shed, walking quietly, watching the rear of the store. He walked directly toward the side of the store away from the stream, and when he was in its lee, he paused to listen. He caught the faint sound of someone whistling in the street, and he moved on along the side of the building, halting at the corner of the porch.

The whistling was close now. In the background was the sound of sweeping too, and he peered carefully around the corner of the building.

A swamper was lackadaisically moving a broom across the boards of the porch. He was a bent wreck of a man in middle age, and from the points of his shoulders, his soiled clothes seemed to sag their way down his body to his very boots, which were trampling the cuffs of his pants. His whistle was oddly cheerful, and Moffat was of mind to greet him when he saw the swamper look off toward the creek. Giving the creek and trail a careful scanning, the man returned to his sweeping.

Moffat paid him a sharp attention, suspicion tugging at him. The swamper was working the same spot over and over with his broom, and again he glanced toward the creek.

A faint surge of excitement came to Moffat then. This swamper could be Arnie's lookout, posted here to warn him of Moffat's approach. If so, Arnie was inside.

There was no chance of surprise now, Moffat knew, and he did not like this. But he hesitated only a moment, then moved. Quietly, he swung up onto the porch, and he was over the rail and halfway across the porch before the swamper turned and saw him. The whistling ceased.

Moffat leveled his gun, and raised a finger to his lips. The swamper hesitated only a moment, and then said in a clear, overloud voice, "Why are you stickin' that gun at me? I got no money."

Moffat was already wheeling toward the store's open door at his right when he heard the sound from inside. It came from above stairs, the sound of a man running, his feet pounding the floorboards in movement toward the back of the building. Arnie had been in the bunkroom, probably with the lone window open so he could hear his lookout's signal.

Moffat was moving into the big room when he heard the crash of glass, and he hauled up. He remembered then the single window in the upstairs corridor, and he wheeled back out of the room and cut to his left across the porch in the direction from which he had come.

Vaulting the railing he landed heavily in the gravel and fell erect on one knee. His legs were already driving as he came erect, running for the rear of the building.

He was racing full tilt when he approached the corner, and he raised his gun, ready to cut off Arnie's escape. He hugged the corner, rounding it, and then, with the abruptness of a thunderclap, Arnie, running full tilt too, rounded the corner.

Moffat reacted by instinct. He leveled his gun and pulled the trigger as he crashed into Arnie, and the two of them met with a force that drove the breath out of Moffat and sent him in a lunging, turning sprawl into the gravel.

He landed on his side and rolled with his momentum, and then he came to his knees and whirled, swinging his gun in front of him.

But Arnie was down. He lay on his back past the corner and he was drawing up one leg in a tight turning motion against his belly.

Moffat rose unsteadily, and hung his head, gagging for breath, his gun hanging loosely at his side, watching Arnie. When, seconds later, he walked unsteadily in Arnie's direction, Arnie did not move.

Moffat heard the rear door of the store open, and the swarthy bartender tentatively poked his head out. He looked carefully at Moffat and Moffat halted, breathing deeply, and looked carefully at him.

Moffat said, "You want any part of this?" in a voice hard with truculence. The bartender's head disappeared,

130

and Moffat walked over to Arnie and stood above him. He had shot Arnie in the chest. A piece of Arnie's shirt was smoking where the powder from Moffat's shot had set it afire.

Moffat knelt beside him, thinking wryly, *I shouldn't have shot.* For whatever Arnie knew was safe enough now, Moffat thought, and he laid his gun down in the gravel and pinched out the smoldering sparks of Arnie's shirt. He felt an angry bafflement as he looked at Arnie's face. This was the end of it, expressed in the oddly gentle mockery of the dead.

With only a faint hope of finding out anything that would help him, Moffat rolled him over and began to go through his pockets. The contents of one was eloquent enough—the heel of plug of twist, an unpolished garnet, and a limp purse that held a single silver dollar.

The other pocket held a knife, a religious medallion, and another purse, worn and smooth. As soon as he hefted this, Moffat frowned. Opening it, he dumped the contents in his palm. Ten double eagles tumbled in his palm, and Moffat stared at them. Two purses, one with a dollar in it, the other with two hundred dollars. *The first one Arnie's, the second pay for killing me?* he wondered.

And then he thought, *Bill Taff paid him once.* He came to his feet, frowning. *Maybe Charlie, though,* he thought, remembering Charlie's presence at the bridge. He didn't know. But it was a safe assumption that Arnie hadn't made the attempt on his own initiative. Arnie, broke, would never seek revenge, but Arnie, with two hundred dollars pay, might be pleased to.

Afterward, Moffat left Arnie and went in the store. To the bartender, who was the owner too, he explained his wants. Food, the rental of a fresh horse, and a burial of sorts for Arnie could all be arranged for one of the double eagles Moffat offered him.

Moffat ate his breakfast in the dirty kitchen at the rear of the store while the swamper retrieved his horse and put his saddle on a fresh mount, and it was scarcely an hour after sunup when he was again on the trail, headed back for Vermilion.

With the warm sun on his back and food in his belly, Moffat felt his weariness. But the purse in his pocket, heavy against his leg, was a goad to speculation. An overwhelming and tenacious desire to settle this was riding him. Sleep could wait. *Charlie or Taff?* he kept wondering. All morning, as the back trail lifted to the peaks, he tirelessly turned over in his mind these two names. But when he would settle the guilt on Taff, memory of Charlie's threats rose to confound him. And when he favored Charlie, as he did many times, memory of Taff's treacheries made him doubt himself.

The clear, cloudless day made the negotiation of the pass almost pleasant. On the far slope, the utter stillness of the timber and the sun overhead made him drowse.

It was then that it happened. He was roused by the chill shade of high pines and far ahead of him he saw sunlight again and the trail angle around a high, sunlit shoulder of rock.

Once in the sun, he felt sleep stealing upon him.

The shot, the heavy blow on his shoulder, the noise came all at once. He was driven out of the saddle by the force against his shoulder, and he was full awake as he felt his horse shying from under him.

It was only when he had fallen heavily, had felt the taste of dirt in his mouth, that he acknowledged bleakly, *I made a mistake.*

7

HE WAS gathering himself to rise, feeling the wild urgency in him to find his feet and face the ambusher, when the cold and dismal realization came to him. He was lying belly down on the open trail, and his horse had shied clear of him. The smallest movement on his part would invite the second shot, this time at the broad of his back.

He lay utterly still then, his face still in the dirt, feeling the skin of his back crawling, feeling time slow down, and stop. He knew then that the two seconds it had taken him to sum up his situation had irrevocably committed him to this ruse. He must feign death until the ambusher was off guard.

132

His left arm, which was under him, was numb and had no feeling in itself, but he felt a warm wetness against his upper chest, and he knew this was blood.

He became acutely aware of the slightest sound, and he listened with an agonizing intensity for any sound of movement against rock. For he was certain that his ambusher was hidden in the rocks to the left of the trail above him.

But there was no telltale sound. He heard his horse moving slowly across the trail, heard him pull at the wayside grass, heard the far-off scolding of a squirrel and overhead the snooping flight of a jay; he heard his own pulse hammering with a violence that he was sure was shaking his body. No other sound came to him, and he thought, *Is he waiting me out?* Again he felt the cold crawling sensation on his back, and he began to sweat with fear.

And then, after an eternity, he heard the sound he had been waiting for—the sound of boots moving upon rock. Instantly, he beat his memory for the shape of the rock, and he seemed to remember, drowsy as he had been, that the trail face of the rock was too steep to climb. That meant his ambusher must descend another face of it.

And now he listened as if his very life depended upon the accuracy of his hearing. The bootsteps were moving tentatively, and he thought, *He's looking for a way down.* Then the sound ceased, there was a moment of silence, and he heard it again, this time muffled by distance, and he thought, *Now!*

He exploded into movement then, his legs driving him onto all fours. But he had miscalculated, and put his weight on his numb arm. Pain knifed through his shoulder, and the arm gave way and he fell heavily upon it. A searching jolt of pain pushed a cry to his throat, but he rolled flat on his belly and with his good arm pushed himself erect. He was already running toward the downtrail face of the rock, yanking the gun from his belt and cocking it with his good hand.

He left the trail for the rise of the talus at the base of the rock, driving for the rounded corner of it ten feet ahead. His footing slipped once and he fell to his knee, and then he was up and lunging forward again.

He rounded the corner abruptly and halted, and then

lifted his gaze to the face of the boulder. There, ten feet above him and clinging to footholds on the rock face was Charlie Storrs. Oblivious to Moffat, he was carefully descending, hampered somewhat by the six-gun held in his right hand.

It took Moffat one stunned moment to recognize him, during which his upswinging gun halted. Then the wild rage came, and Moffat called thinly, "You should have shot twice, Charlie."

Storrs' head swiveled, and instantly he pushed away from the rock and jumped, half turning in mid-air. His hands were held high above his head in the balancing position instinctive to a jumping man.

As he landed heavily in the talus rubble, his weight beating him to his knees, his gun came down with a clubbing motion and he shot swiftly, with a wild urgency, and missed.

Moffat shot too, as if by reflex, and he heard his bullet smash the rock above Charlie's head. Now Charlie was rising, lunging across the eight feet of space toward him, and Moffat shot again.

Charlie's back bowed with a jerk, and his forward leg, accepting his driving weight, buckled sideways, so that he turned as he fell. Rolling over twice more, he came to rest on his back at Moffat's feet.

Moffat saw the hole in his throat pouring out its torrent of blood, and he turned away, sickened.

He moved back and sank down on the talus slope and carefully cradled his useless arm in his lap. Looking obliquely at Charlie now, he said aloud, without anger, "You fool. You poor fool."

He was trembling, and he closed his eyes and hung his head for a moment, afterwards taking a deep and shuddering breath. When he looked up again, the noon was sunlit, still as a pool, its tranquillity strangely unmarred by this violence. His arm ached steadily, but for the moment he paid it no attention. The shock at discovering Charlie was the bushwacker was still with him. That Charlie could kill in hot blood he had never doubted. But this way, never.

Now the pieces of the puzzle began to fit, and putting them together was simple enough. It was Charlie who had paid the gold to Arnie, and who was waiting at the bridge for confirmation of Moffat's death. And Charlie, seeing Arnie had failed, had resolved to finish it himself.

It need never have happened, Moffat knew, if Josephine had been a good wife. Her discontent had bred the jealousy that killed her husband. Thinking of her, Moffat felt only a vast pity.

The insistent throbbing of his arm roused him to movement. His left sleeve was wet with blood, and gently now, he felt of the wound. The shot had angled down through the thick part of his upper arm; the long muscle of his bicep felt shredded and torn and sore, though the bone was untouched.

He rose wearily, and moved off across the trail into the pine timber. Moving about, he gathered the small streamers of moss hanging from the dead lower branches of the pines, and when he had enough he plastered the moss against the wound and bound it firmly with his handkerchief.

Afterward, he caught his horse down the trail and, teetering with weariness, read his choice. He could spend the last of his strength scouting for Charlie's horse, loading the body and bringing it to camp late tonight, or he could make it alone with daylight to spare.

He thought of Charlie, then, waiting the long, dragging hours atop the rock, patient in the knowledge that he was going to shoot a man in the back.

Moffat mounted and rode on alone.

Dutch pushed the half-filled glass of whiskey away from him, and wheeled restlessly away from the bar. It was the midafternoon lull in the Comfort, and a pair of idle miners were playing blackjack at one of the tables, the only men in the saloon besides himself and the bartender.

Dutch cruised over toward them and, changing his mind, veered off and came to a morose halt before one of the big windows. He didn't want a drink, he couldn't work, and he didn't feel like eating. He couldn't go home and face Candace with the news that Larkin hadn't shown up yet, and he couldn't stand sitting home and waiting. *And watching her,* he thought grimly.

He recalled without pleasure his return home in the small hours of this morning. The look on her face, when she saw Larkin was not with him, had sickened his heart.

135

He had seen that look on the faces of women before, when, after a big accident in the workings, they waited at the tunnel mouth for their men to come out.

The trouble was, he thought, that she had communicated her fear to him. It was Arnie, so the story went around town, whom Moffat had taken out after. But where was he? How long did it take to catch a man, or miss him? Every hour was adding to Dutch's pessimism.

He looked down absently at the ore sample on the sill, feeling a wild restlessness take hold of him. Moving now, he opened the door and mounted the steps and stood teetering on the top plank, his gaze raking the street both ways for any sign of Moffat.

He swore out loud then, without any passion or cause, and afterward stared moodily at the hotel front across the street. The question that had been floating in the back of his mind all morning, bobbed up again now. It took the same form as before and was just as unanswerable as before—*Is the damn stuff worth this?* Was all the ore he was getting out of Big Jay, the fabulous bank account that would accrue from it, worth Moffat's death? To answer that, all he needed to do was remember the look on Candace's face. She was in love with Larkin, and if he were killed all the money in all the mines in the country couldn't make it up to Candace.

A miner passed in front of him now, saying, "Hiya' Dutch," and Dutch said "Fine," and looked at the man and added belatedly, "Pete," and immediately forgot him.

He allowed himself to speculate on just what he wanted out of this money. He wanted the money to buy him the fun of turning up other good prospects, but beyond that, or before it, he wanted it to buy Candace everything she wanted. *But she knows what she wants,* Dutch thought grimly, *and it's got nothing to do with money.*

His glance unconsciously strayed past the corner of the hotel to Jarboe's office up the hill and he looked away, wondering, remembering last night. When he'd left Candace at the hotel last night, he'd gone straight to the Comfort and found Bill Taff there. Taff had been there all evening, the bartender had told him. But later, the conviction had come to Dutch, and was still with him, that Arnie hadn't shot at Moffat without some expert

136

prodding from Taff or Jarboe. They'd bought Arnie once when Spence was beat up; they could buy him again.

Dutch groaned softly then and, hearing himself, he looked around to see if others had heard him. He was still alone, the lazy noon traffic idling past him.

Suddenly, he knew the time for decision was here, and the time for pride past.

He stepped out into the road and heard a sharp swearing. Looking up, he saw the team almost atop him, and he dodged swiftly back. As the wagon dragged past him the teamster called down,, "Sleep at home, Dutch."

"Ah-h-h," Dutch snarled. He waited with a vast impatience until the wagon was past, and then he cut across the street, touched the hotel corner, and angled up the hill toward Jarboe's office.

Stepping in the open door out of the sunlight, he halted. The sight of Jarboe seated in his swivel chair, back to desk, talking with Bill Taff slouched in the wall chair, brought a surge of anger to him. Knowing this was a luxury he could not allow himself, he was silent a moment, controlling himself. Bill Taff, sensing trouble, came swiftly out of his chair.

Jarboe, however, showed no alarm, and said affably, "Afternoon, Dutch."

Dutch said, then, "I want to call it quits, R. B."

Jarboe came erect in his chair with quick, feline attentiveness. His comprehension lagged, however, for the surprise that washed over him was genuine, and Dutch beheld it with a feeling of bitter irony.

"Quits?" Jarboe asked blankly. "You mean, give up your lease?"

"That's right," Dutch said grimly.

He watched Jarboe's quick glance of suspicion at Taff, and Jarboe regarded him cautiously. "You're offering to sell it to us, are you?"

"I'm offering to tear it up!" Dutch said angrily.

Jarboe looked at him in stunned amazement, speechless a long moment. Belief refused to come to him, Dutch saw. Now Jarboe said, "In exchange for what, Dutch?"

"There's a string, all right," Dutch agreed, "but it's one that shouldn't bother you. You'll have your lease back, and you'll have your fortune." He paused, and then

137

said slowly, "It's this: I want you to leave Moffat alone —for keeps."

The relief on Jarboe's face was like the sun breaking through clouds. "Leave him alone? Why, I've got nothing against him, nothing at all—except he's quarrelsome. But I'll leave him alone." He smiled genially and rose: "Did you bring the lease with you, Dutch?"

"There's a string tied to my string, too," Dutch said.

Jarboe waited and Dutch said, "I'll tear up the lease when Moffat's back here, safe and sound."

Jarboe's fleeting expression was one of indefinable anguish; he looked at the chair he had just vacated, and then gently sat down in it, and then he asked, "Back from where, Dutch?"

A raw anger came to Dutch then and he said, "Damn your gall, Jarboe! I don't know where Larkin is! I think you hired Arnie to kill him! I don't know if he's alive or not, or if you've shot him or had him shot or slugged or knifed! All I know is, if you know where he is you better get him back here—and standing up and breathing, too.'

"But I don't know where he is," Jarboe protested. "How could I bring him back if I don't know that?"

"That's the string," Dutch said implacably.

He turned to go, and Jarboe bolted out of his chair saying, "Hold on, Dutch!" Dutch halted and turned and Jarboe came up to him. Dutch could see the perspiration beading his forehead, and the agony of doubt in his eyes was genuine. "Do I *have* to bring him back, deliver him to you?" Jarboe asked. "If he just comes back, will you tear up the lease?"

"I will," Dutch said. And then his own misgivings, his own pride, pushed him into truculent speech. "Don't think I'm afraid of you, R. B., both of you, all of you!" He glanced wickedly at Taff. "It's just that my ore isn't worth a good man's murder, that's all." He brushed past Jarboe and went out.

Jarboe followed him to the door and gently closed it behind him. Then he turned and looked at Taff, and Taff saw the despair, the temper, the greed in the old man's face.

"Could he be alive?" Jarboe asked.

Taff felt a smothering wrath in him, and he did not answer. He had just heard Dutch Surrency blast any

138

hope he had of sharing the Big Jay pocket with Jarboe—unless Moffat were already dead. He said thinly, then, "You made a bargain and you'll keep it," and walked slowly across the room to Jarboe.

"Not if he's alive!" Jarboe shrilled. "Not if he's alive, I won't! I keep the whole pocket if he's alive!"

"If Arnie's got him, you'll keep your bargain," Taff said implacably.

"Right! Yes! I will!" Jarboe said angrily, and he and Taff watched each other a moment, hating each other. Then Jarboe walked around him and came back to his chair and turned it toward his desk. He put both elbows on the desk top and placed his head in his hands for a moment. Taff watched him sullenly.

Jarboe leaned back in his chair and glanced obliquely at Taff then, his eyes speculative and hard. He repeated his question, "Could he be alive?"

"I thought you didn't want to know anything about it," Taff sneered.

"I don't!" Jarboe said sharply. "But thanks to your damned fumbling, I do know something about it. The whole town does. You hired Arnie?"

Taff nodded sullenly.

"And he missed. I heard that too. Do you think he's killed Moffat, or Moffat's killed him?"

The question was one that had been riding Taff all day, pushing his temper and turning him surly, first with anger and then with a premonition of disaster. He did not answer now, but slowly tramped the length of the room, oblivious to the old man, lost in thought.

He saw the choice before him now with a bitter clarity. Thanks to Dutch's offer to tear up his lease, if he let Moffat return safely he would lose his promised stake. Or he could throw caution to the winds, make a try for Moffat, and, if successful, win his stake that Jarboe must pay him. The risks, so important before Dutch's offer, were not important at all, now. Time was short. Somewhere, on the trail to Weed or in Weed he should find Moffat, and he must leave him dead.

He wheeled now and started for the door. Jarboe came out of his chair as if propelled, and stepped in front of the door, barring his way.

Taff halted, and said in flat finality, "I'll tell you once. Get out of my way."

"You go out that door and I'll ride for Sheriff Halloran," Jarboe countered.

Taff's temper leveled off and, seeing the wild determination in Jarboe's face, knowing the old man had guessed his intentions, he hesitated.

"Don't you go after him, Bill. Even if you got him, even if I paid you, you'd hang, because I'll turn you up," Jarboe said gently.

"That's bluff," Taff said.

Jarboe stepped aside, saying mildly, "Is it? Go ahead."

Taff put out his hand for the doorknob, and then his hand paused, and he looked searchingly at Jarboe. The sobering thought came to him now that if he killed Moffat and the old man turned him up to Halloran, neither in flight nor jail nor death could he enforce payment of the stake Jarboe promised him.

Jarboe said mildly, "Your bet's down, Bill. Let it ride. Neither of us knows if Moffat's alive. Your chance of winning is just as good as mine."

Taff considered this with a reluctant carefulness and saw the wisdom of it. If Moffat were dead, he was safe and rich, and the fact that Moffat had been gone almost twenty-four hours favored that assumption. But to make sure he was dead would involve risks out of all proportion to the gain—if he got the gain. The old man was right. *But damn him,* Taff thought helplessly, wickedly, and his hand fell to his side. He had an almost overpowering impulse to smash Jarboe in the face, but he checked himself and turned away.

He heard Jarboe's soft chuckle, heard him say, "If a man's too sharp, Bill, he always cuts his own throat," and he thought with a cold hatred now, *Some day I'll get you in a corner, old man.*

When Moffat came to the Vermilion road in late afternoon, he crossed it and continued upon the trail that followed the Bone. During the long afternoon, all his thoughts had become centered on one idea, to reach Surrency's cabin. He had clung doggedly to that desire, excluding everything else from his mind, and the creek trail was the shortest route to fulfillment. His arm pained him always, and he had found no way of steadying it
140

against the constant motion of his body in the saddle. His hunger, his weariness, were all submerged in that everlasting wash of pain.

When he was below town, he turned off the trail through the alders of the creek bottom, and presently came into Surrency's clearing at about the spot he judged Arnie had shot at him. He kneed his horse toward the shed and corral and was scarcely past the house when he heard the door open.

He reined up as Candace ran out the door toward him, calling, "Larkin, Larkin!" in a voice that was close to breaking.

She came up to him then and put a hand on his coat, and he looked down at her, smiling, and said, "I took a long ride, Candace," in a voice that was rusty from disuse. Watching her, now, he saw her move her head to the side and downwards, hiding her face from him, and he knew the sight of him had brought tears of relief. He touched her hand and feeling it, she glanced up, smiling, unsteadily.

"You're all right?" she asked.

"Three-quarters all right," Moffat said, and then added wryly, "I would like to get off this damned horse."

Candace ducked under the horse's neck and reached her hands up to help him, and only then saw the bloody sleeve, and the bloody bandage on his upper arm. She stood grave-eyed and motionless, holding the bridle, as Moffat slowly swung out of the saddle, grunting a long, sighing "Ah," as his legs accepted his weight.

Candace reached out now to steady him, and he leaned a moment against her, and then wordlessly turned toward the cabin. Candace walked beside him, helping him, and then at the door, hurried past him and pulled out a chair from the table and watched him settle gently into it.

He leaned back, then, with his useless left arm dangling and Candace circled the chair so that she stood in front of him. There was a look of doubtfulness, of concern, in her face, a look of thankfulness too, and then she smiled briefly at him as she moved quickly over to the stove and shoved the kettle forward.

Moffat thought, *Get it over with,* and he said gently, "Candace, I killed Charlie Storrs."

Candace turned and watched him a moment, her glance searching his face for a clue to his feelings. He grimaced faintly and tiredly scrubbed a hand over his beardstubble, thinking. *He shot at me, didn't he?* But he knew he was voicing this defense only to something in himself that regretted Charlie Storrs' death, not to an accusation in her glance.

Candace came slowly to him now, saying, "Around here, they're saying it was Arnie you took out after, Larkin."

"And Arnie, too," Moffat said wearily.

"Oh, my dear," Candace murmured, putting a soft pity and anguish in the words. Moffat glanced at her in time to see the slight, quick shake of her head from side to side, as if she were checking the emotion welling into her throat. She turned abruptly back to the stove, and she was pouring hot water into a basin when she said, "Do you want to tell me about it?"

He didn't want to, and he thought of this a moment while she put the basin on the table and got her scissors and began cutting the stiff sleeve away from his arm. And then he knew he must, because this was a part of her too, as it would be a part of Dutch and all of them.

Tonelessly, still without liking it, he told her of cornering Arnie in Weed, and of finding the money in his pocket. And then, because his mind was tired and forgetful of details, he had to go back and tell her of meeting Charlie Storrs at the bridge, and of his suspicion afterward. Continuing, he told of his puzzlement as to who had given the gold to Arnie.

The sharp bite of the turpentine that Candace was pouring on his wound checked his speech for a while, and afterwards he finished his account of Charlie's attempt on his life.

The senselessness of Charlie's death came to him again, and his voice grew somber in the telling, and when he finished he glanced up to see Candace watching him intently, her eyes dark with pity.

"That needn't have happened," she said softly. "He needn't have hated you."

"Josephine," Moffat said.

"Yes. There's no other cruelty like that."

142

She finished bandaging his arm and now moved into her room, brought out a shirt of Dutch's, and went back again to her room. He climbed into the shirt, realizing the hammering ache of his arm was diminishing, and he saw that while she had been busy with dressing his hurt, she had moved pans onto the front of the stove too, and he could smell food.

As he was buckling his belt, she returned with a bottle of whiskey and set it and a glass before him, saying, "I always do things backwards, Larkin. This should have been first."

Moffat poured himself a drink and downed it, feeling its hot fire slug life into him. In contented silence now, he watched Candace move about the room preparing his food. He glanced at the window beside the stove and saw the square of cardboard that replaced the pane Arnie's bullet had smashed, and it occurred to him then that he had returned here today as if by instinct. He could not remember thinking of any other place. And Candace had accepted his return in the same way, as if there were no other place he would go for help and for comfort.

He remembered the time, numbered in days but a lifetime distant, when even knowing Candace and Dutch had been an unwanted thing, and burdensome. Now he had come full circle, so that he could not imagine his life without her, and he remembered the things he had wanted to say to her last night, and that he had not said because Dutch and Spence had interrupted him. And he could not say them now, because there was one thing more he must do, a chore he did not relish.

Candace moved to the table with his food. Part of the deer Manahan had given them she had boiled with barley into a plain Indian stew that Moffat wolfed hungrily. Candace sat across the table from him watching him, cutting his meat for him, telling of their search for him in the brush last night, of Dutch's restless impatience, and finally, of Spence's return to work at the Big Jay today while Dutch shirked it, waiting for word of him.

Afterward, when Candace had packed his pipe and he had lighted it, he rose, and Candace with him. She carried the few dishes to the sink, and Moffat tramped over to the door and looked out. He saw his horse, which he had forgotten, grazing in the brush. He turned him into the corral, and with difficulty removed the saddle and bridle, and closed the corral gate.

Walking back to the house, he knew he could put this off no longer. Stepping inside, he took down his hat and coat from the nail where they had hung since last night, and went over to Candace at the table, extending his coat.

She looked up at him questioningly, and he said, "There's Dutch to find. There's something else, too."

"Yes, there's Josephine to tell," Candace said. She took the coat and helped him on with it, and when he turned to face her, he read the unspoken sympathy for him in her eyes.

He asked, curiously, "In one way or another, she's always been between us, hasn't she, Candace?"

Candace nodded, almost imperceptibly.

"Not any more. Not after this," he said quietly, and reached out and took her hand. "I want——" he began, and his voice trailed off.

Candace watched him, and a deep and womanly wisdom touched her expression as she waited for him to go on.

"Afterwards," he said, then, and smiled gently and let go of her arm, and his glance lingered on her a moment before he turned and went out. This was no time to tell her or try to make her understand that carrying this word to Josephine signified the end of something in his life, and that he wanted it over with before he spoke. It was the ending of Josephine and Charlie, of Corona and the dismal years of shame and hiding, and of the bitter gall of false pride. He wanted it out of the way and done with.

He took the trail back through the thicket at a slow pace, partly because his legs were unsteady, partly because of a deep reluctance to face Josephine. When he reached the main street, and cut across the road toward the hotel, the millhands and teamsters were tramping down the hill. The town was stirring with movement, and the din of the Silverbell's piano blanketed the four corners. Moffat spoke to a couple of men, who eyed knowingly the empty sleeve of his coat, but he did not stop.

He went into the hotel and inquired for Mrs. Storrs and was told she was in her room, and he mounted the

144

tairs. Pausing at the head of the stair well, he looked down the corridor at the door of her room. The tag ends of unwelcome memories crowded into his mind now, memories of Josephine and that other life, and now he moved, wanting to get this finished.

Josephine answered his knock. When she saw who it was she instinctively started toward him, and then checked herself, and stood with her hand on the knob, not speaking immediately. Moffat saw she had sensed something amiss. The dark suit she was wearing gave her a curious regality against the twilit dusk of her room, and she moved aside and said, "Come inside, Larkin," and Moffat stepped in.

She touched his empty coat sleeve as he passed, and then quickly shut the door and came to him, so that when he halted she was before him.

"What is it, Larkin? You're hurt. Did—" she halted, not knowing what to ask first or say next, and her eyes were searching his face, quietly imploring.

Moffat thought, *There's no easy way to say it,* and he said levelly, "Josephine, Charlie is dead. I killed him."

She stood utterly still, accepting this, then she ceased looking at his eyes, but looked at his face, and then his chin, and then his shirt, and finally, after a long time, at her hands folded in front of her. It was a slow withdrawal of acceptance, a turning away from a brutal fact, a steeling of will.

She said in a flat voice, "I knew it would happen."

At that moment Moffat felt it hard to pity her, and he said with an irony he could not help, "Yes, a man has to die sometime. But not always that way."

Her glance raised to him briefly and slid away, and then it returned to him, bold now. "What you mean is that I'm not saying what I should, or acting as I should; me, a widow."

"Yes."

"And I won't," she said promptly. "I am more glad you're alive than sorry Charlie's dead, if that makes sense, Larkin."

He said nothing, and she half turned from him, and said in a low voice, "Now you understand that, tell me what happened." She glanced briefly over her shoulder and said, "Charlie left me last night. He told me he never

145

wanted to see me again—if that will make your mind any easier."

Moffat ignored that. He told what had happened in less detail than he had told Candace, and while he was talking Josephine sat on the bed, her back bent a little, hands folded in her lap, looking at the floor.

When he finished, she was silent a moment and then, still without looking at him, she said, "I suppose I—he's still up there?"

"I'll take care of that," Moffat said. He could not keep the puzzlement from his voice, and hearing it, Josephine looked up sharply.

She came to her feet, and now, for the first time, Moffat saw some emotion in her face and in her movement.

"Oh, Larkin, *why* must I pretend—especially to you. It isn't as if you'd thought I loved Charlie!"

"No," Moffat agreed.

"Then what shocks you? Why are you looking at me like that?"

Moffat lifted his hat slowly and looked at it, and said in a gentle voice, "I don't know, Josephine. It's just that I'm remembering now that I was a pretty big kid before I quit crying every time I lost a horse." He looked at her now, and said with a biting mildness, "But that's not the same thing, is it?"

The twilight had deepened so that he could not tell if she blushed. He was suddenly weary of this, suddenly aware, too, of the wish to hurt her. She had shared a man's life and hopes and ambitions for three years, and now she had accepted his death as a pool accepts a stone, with a ripple that dies as it is watched.

She came off the bed now, saying gently, "You don't understand much of a woman's thoughts, do you, Larkin?"

"Not much."

"They're seldom confused, like yours are now."

Moffat said nothing, wondering what was coming.

Josephine came close to him now, and her expression was sober. "Mine haven't been confused at all, not since you and I met. The thought that colored my whole life was that I loved you and wanted to be your wife. When I couldn't be, I compromised, as a woman will. The compromise didn't mean anything. The end of it doesn't either."

"All right," Larkin said tiredly.

"My thoughts aren't confused yet, not even now, Larkin. I'm free now, and I——"

Moffat's voice rode down her words as he said sharply, "Don't say it, Josephine. That's done!"

She watched him silently a moment, as if confirming a knowledge she already had, and then she said bitterly, "If I'd wept over Charlie, it would have made a difference, wouldn't it?"

"No."

"Then you just plain hate me, don't you, Larkin?" he asked then.

Moffat sighed. "No."

And now Josephine's voice took on a dry, thrusting timbre. "Or is it that you just plain love that Surrency girl?"

Temper flared in Moffat then, and seeing it in his eyes, Josephine smiled in malice. The temper died and Moffat said mildly, "You said that once before, Josephine. I couldn't answer you, because I wasn't sure. Now I am. Yes, you're right."

"How romantic," Josephine gibed. Her lips were crooked, jeering, and she said then, in the same derisive way, "That little kitchen drab! And she's rich, too. Can you keep her out of the kitchen after you marry her, Larkin?"

A faint amusement touched Moffat then. Josephine had made her try and now, after her fashion, wanted to hurt him in revenge. He said dryly, pleasantly, "You're marrying me off, Josephine. I don't even know if she'll have me."

"You blind idiot; she told me she loved you. She's only praying you'll ask her."

"Told you?" Moffat asked sharply. "When?"

"Last night when she came here to blame Charlie for shooting at you through the window."

The ghost of a smile touched Moffat's lips, and then he murmured, "Thank you, Josephine," and moved past her. He halted then, remembering, and rammed his hand in his pocket and brought out Charlie's purse he had taken from Arnie.

147

Extending it to her, he said, "You should have this."

Josephine looked at him suspiciously, and then at the purse. "What is it?"

"Charlie's purse. I found it in Arnie's pocket. I suppose it's what Charlie paid him to kill me."

She made no effort to take it, only raised her glance to him and then, even in the half light of dusk, he saw the fury in her face.

She struck the purse out of his hand with a savage bat of her palm, and he looked at her in amazement. She brushed past him then to the bureau, pulled out a drawer, and reached inside. She brought out something and held it out to him, and looking down at it, he saw it was a purse.

"This is Charlie's purse! He gave it to me last night when he told me to leave him!" She closed her palm on it and then said wickedly, wrathfully, "You don't have to buy me off, you clumsy fool!"

For the two full seconds it took Moffat to comprehend this, he stared at her. Then he knelt, picked up the purse, and without looking at her or speaking to her, he went out, closing the door behind him.

At the head of the stairs, under the lamp that had been lighted since he came, he halted and looked at the purse, the significance of Josephine's last words shaping slowly and terribly in his mind. *This was not Charlie's purse.* If it had been his, or an old one that he no longer carried, Josephine would have recognized it. She would never have rejected it and wrathfully misconstrued his return of it if she had ever seen it before.

His hand closed slowly over the purse, and he patiently thought back. He had assumed, after Charlie's try at him, that Charlie had hired Arnie. But in the face of this evidence, he'd been wrong. Charlie knew where he was going and had seen him go. Wild with jealousy, he could have seen his opportunity to murder and go free, since Moffat's death would be laid to Arnie. Then who *had* paid Arnie?

The thought came to him instantly. *Bill Taff. He paid him two dollars for a beating. Why not two hundred for a killing?* He waited a moment longer, considering, and all the time his conviction was deepening. Slowly, he

ipped the purse back in his pocket, and now he knew
hat was before him and what must be done.

He took the stairs carefully, and at the bottom of them
e turned toward the desk. Mrs. Barber, massive in a
esh dress, was sitting behind the counter, and when he
ame up she smiled.

She rose now, her face jolly and telling of her eager-
ess to talk, and Moffat cut in ahead of her. "Mrs. Bar-
er, has Tim got a gun in the house?"

Mrs. Barber's face altered instantly in soberness. She
oked searchingly at him, and seeing his face, she said
berly, "We keep one behind the desk here."

"May I have it?" Moffat asked.

Mrs. Barber reached down and got the six-gun and
id it on the counter. Wordlessly, Moffat glanced at it
d checked its loads, and rammed it in his belt, saying,
Thank you," as he turned away.

A pair of men in the lobby chairs looked oddly at him
s he went out. On the steps he paused, and moved aside
r some men mounting the steps, and he looked over the
wn, thinking, *He won't run. There's that about him.*

Walking down the steps, he turned upstreet and cut
round the corner of the hotel. Halfway up the hill, he
uld see Jarboe's office, and he saw that it was dark. He
alted, glancing up at the mill, and saw that it was dark,
o, and he was standing there irresolute when he heard
s name called.

Turning, he saw Dutch hurrying toward him. Dutch
id, "Well, you're walking and talking," and put out his
nd and Moffat took it, smiling a little.

Dutch said, "What happened? Does Candace know?"

"She knows," Moffat said.

"You're hurt," Dutch said. "What happened?"

Moffat drew a deep breath, and said, "Dutch, I haven't
t time to tell you," and he looked past Dutch at the
verbell and then to the Comfort. Then he said,
Where's Bill Taff?"

"No," Dutch said promptly. "No. Don't do it. You
n't have to."

Moffat peered at him in the dusk, a look of wonder-
ent in his face, and Dutch said, "It's all over. I'm tear-
g up the lease, Larkin."

149

"Why?"

"I'm rich enough. It's not worth this."

Moffat was silent a moment, and then he asked meagrely, "Have you torn it up, Dutch?"

"No."

"Don't," Moffat said, and moved past him down the hill. Dutch started to follow him, and Moffat said over his shoulder, "Stay clear of this, Dutch," and he heard Dutch halt. He walked on alone, now, heading for the Comfort. There weren't many places in town to look, and the Comfort was as good a place to start as any.

The room was crowded as he stepped inside, with the gambling tables crowded, the bar less so.

He was halfway across the room before he saw Taff and Jarboe standing at the bar, and turning toward them he thought, *The old man can watch it, too.*

He came up beside Jarboe and put a foot on the rail and the bartender leaned forward.

"Whiskey," Moffat said. At the sound of his voice Jarboe turned, and when he saw Moffat he smiled cordially, his glance touching Moffat's empty sleeve and sliding away.

"Why, hello, son," the old man said. "Glad you're back. Have you seen Dutch?"

"I saw him," Moffat said. His glance shifted to Taff who was carefully toying with his drink, looking at it.

Jarboe said, "Let me buy you a drink."

"It's my treat," Moffat said. He reached in his pocket and brought out the purse and tossed it on the bar. The coins chinked heavily as the purse landed in front of Jarboe. Moffat said gently, "Pay him for me, will you?"

He saw Jarboe look at the purse, and then become utterly still, and he glanced at Taff and saw his fingers cease playing with the glass and become quiet as he looked at the purse. Taff's glance lifted first; it barely touched Moffat and settled on the old man. Jarboe reached out slowly for the purse, and then changed his mind, looking at it in bemused concentration.

Moffat said again gently, "Ever see it before?"

Jarboe didn't move. Taff eased slowly erect, and Moffat felt the break gathering, and he moved his hand on the bar.

150

And then Taff spoke with a cold and calculated malice.
I have. It's Jarboe's."

Jarboe's head jerked up; he hesitated only long enough
comprehend his betrayal and then he lunged at Taff,
narling curses.

Moffat plunged away from the bar, his hand streaking
or the gun in his belt, hearing the stampede of the other
en away from the bar. He saw Taff push away from the
ar too, and Jarboe was on him, beating savagely at his
ace with one hand and clawing with the other.

Moffat's gun was out, up and cocked now, but Jarboe
as between him and Taff, and Taff's gun was almost
lear when Jarboe lunged for it. Taff stepped back,
ursing savagely, and as his gun came free he shot. Jar-
oe simply folded his arms around his belly and sat down,
nd now Taff, a wild knowledge in him that he was too
te, swung up his gun, cocking it.

He was already in Moffat's sight, and Moffat squeezed
ne trigger. He saw Taff half turn, and now Moffat shot
gain, again carefully, and he saw Taff turn fully as he
ll, so that his face rapped the bar rail with a muffled
olidity. Jarboe tried to move a frail hand, failed, and
y still.

Moffat lowered his gun in the trailing seconds of
ilence, and then he moved toward the bar. He rammed
ne gun in his belt and reached for the purse, looking at
ne bartender.

"Halloran knows where I am," he said, and turned and
aced the crowd. For a brief moment, he eyed any man
ho would look at him, and then moved toward the
oor. The swell of talk burst after him, and he slowly
ounted the steps. He looked around for Dutch, then,
nd could not see him, and oddly, now, it seemed very
ecessary to return Tim Barber's gun.

He crossed the street and left the gun with Mrs. Barber
the desk, and went out again. Men were running for
e Comfort now. They passed him, and he went on in
ne deep dusk past the Comfort and down the hill, leav-
g the road for the trail through the alder thicket.

He heard her running before he could see her, and he
aited, and when she came around the thicket and saw
m, she did not hesitate.

He held out his arm, and when she came to him, clos to him, clinging to his coat, he held her tightly until he trembling diminished.

He said then, "You couldn't have heard it, clear dow here."

"Dad came home. He saw it," Candace whispered.

Moffat smiled into the night and he said gently, "Sto] shaking. I want to talk to you."

ABOUT THE AUTHOR

LUKE SHORT, whose real name was Frederick D. Glidden, was born in Illinois in 1907. Before devoting himself to writing westerns, he was a trapper in the Canadian Subarctic, worked as an assistant to an archeologist, and was a newsman. Because he believed that an author can write best about the places he knows most intimately, he located his westerns on familiar ground. He was an avid skier and mountain explorer, and lived in Colorado until his death in 1975.